## ABOUT THIS BOOK

**This sequel to *Dawn of the Witch Hunters* by *USA Today* bestselling author Morgan Wylie continues the story of Marie and Judson.**

Marie Blackstone is settling into her new life with Judson Carter in the beautiful box canyon they now call home. On a constant quest to prove her legitimacy—especially to the witches—Marie goes to great lengths to follow a feeling she's only encountered once before and hoped never to again. Someone's practicing the dark arts, but she can't quite discern who.

Within their growing settlement, darkness has found its way through the town's protective wards. And it seems to have an insatiable thirst for magic—witch magic. When witches begin to disappear or turn up drained of their magic, suspicion and fear grow. And some are looking at Marie, the resident witch hunter.

Finding her powers inconsistent and unreliable, Marie struggles to believe in herself and trust her abilities, especially as members of the town begin to doubt her. If she can't find and destroy the black magic and save the witches, she could lose the life she fought so hard to find—and ultimately her soul.

# LEGENDS OF HAVENWOOD FALLS BOOKS

*Lost in Time* by Tish Thawer

*Dawn of the Witch Hunters* by Morgan Wylie

*Redemption's End* by Eric R. Asher

*Trapped Within a Wish* by Brynn Myers

*Blood and Damnation* by Belinda Boring

*Fated Beginnings* by E.J. Fechenda

*Emeline* by Katie M. John

*Released From a Curse* by Brynn Myers

*A Pack of Lies* by Kallie Ross

*Kiss the Ashes* by Desiree Lafawn

*Hidden Truths* by Colleen Nye

*Wrath and Retribution* by Belinda Boring

*Changing Fate* by Char Webster

*Rise of the Witch Hunters* by Morgan Wylie

*The Drowning Bride* by Seven Jane

Also try the main Havenwood Falls series; the YA line, Havenwood Falls High; the darker, sexier side of town, Havenwood Falls Sin & Silk; and the local supernatural college, Sun & Moon Academy.

Stay up to date at www.HavenwoodFalls.com

# BOOKS BY MORGAN WYLIE

## YA FANTASY

Silent Orchids (Book 1)

Veiled Shadows (Book 2)

Daegan (Novella 2.5)

Fractured Darkness (Book 3)

Fading Light (Book 4)

The Sol-lumieth (Book 5) (Winter 2019)

The Rise of the Paladin (An Alandria Short Story Prequel) (Free with Newsletter subscription)

## YA PARANORMAL/SUPERNATURAL

HAILEY: The Necromancer (A Shadow Realm Novella 1) (previously released as Supernatural Chronicles: The Necromancers Novella #7)

JAX: The Doppelgänger (A Shadow Realm Novella 2)

WILLOW (A Shadow Realm Novella 3) (Coming soon!)

SOLANGE (A Shadow Realm Novella 4) (Coming soon!)

## NA/ADULT PARANORMAL ROMANCE

RYLEN (The Tangled Web Book 1)

MATHER (The Tangled Web Book 2)

JET (A Tangled Web Novella)

## HAVENWOOD FALLS

Reawakened (A Havenwood Falls High Novella)

# RISE OF THE WITCH HUNTERS

## A LEGENDS OF HAVENWOOD FALLS NOVELLA

## MORGAN WYLIE

*To the Havenwood Falls Book Club and readers . . . You ROCK!*
*Thank you for reading our stories and loving our town as much as*
*we, the authors, do.*

# CHAPTER 1

1858 WHISPER FALLS

*M*arie Blackstone meandered down an aisle, passing through new shoots of grape vines in the oldest section of the Blackstone vineyard. The aroma of the sticky sweet fruit wafted into her nose as she passed by. As she approached the large outbuilding, she expected to run into the waiting arms of her husband, Judson. Except he wasn't standing with the barrels of wine where he was supposed to be. Noting her bare feet, Marie paused and slowly turned her head, realizing she was not alone. She took in the faces of a small crowd of townspeople around her, but something strange happened. Faces distorted and blurred. Her pulse quickened, and she looked around with panic.

*Where's Judson?*

Beyond the blurred faces, trees slowly enclosed around them. Within the trees, Marie spotted something—something she couldn't quite define. Dark wispy shadows of swirling masses wrapped around the trees, moving closer, stretching out tendrils of smoke, and invading the town and the people within it. Marie doubled over. Her stomach hurt so bad with the effects of dark magic she thought she would be sick. Her hands shook. Her head swam with visions of darkness, and dizziness took her down to her knees.

*Judson! Where are you?* Marie screamed but no sound came from her mouth. Her words were trapped in her mind.

Soon the townspeople faded from her view, consumed by the darkness as it moved closer toward her. Silhouettes emerged but not enough to recognize who or what they were. Were they supernatural? Were they creatures of some kind? Were they the souls of people she knew?

Out of nowhere Judson shot out in front of Marie, holding some kind of tool—a small sword with a glowing stone, her family dagger—sending a jolt of light toward the darkness. The light mixed with the power Judson had somehow infused it with and pushed the darkness back with hisses of displeasure screeching through the night.

*Judson! Judson!* Marie called again, but she couldn't seem to reach him with her voice. Instead she reached out her hand to grab his, but he, too, faded away from her with the townspeople. Marie heard words before she also faded into nothingness:

"Release me, Marie."

Then darkness swallowed her.

Marie awoke gasping for air, doubled over in pain. Her brow was slicked with sweat as she opened her eyes and took in the room around her. She pushed back her long blond hair away from her sticky skin. Home. She was in her bed.

A dream. It had all been a dream. Then why did she still feel so sick? Could it also be a warning?

Marie wasn't surprised to not see Judson in bed next to her. Since they'd been married, he'd been busy with blacksmith work.

She called out, her voice dry and scratchy from sleep, "Judson? Are you there?"

When Judson didn't reply, she stumbled to her feet and went in search of him. The more she moved, the more she felt herself coming back from the brink of whatever ailment she had experienced. Her heart rate slowed to normal, and her breathing finally caught up with her. She had only felt a feeling so strong once before, when she and Judson had traveled across the country by wagon train with the other original settlers. They had stumbled upon an encampment of witches—witches who had been performing black magic. Unfortunately, her brother Dante and his band of rogue witch hunters had killed them all before she arrived and had the chance to stop him. He had been sending her a message: *This is our calling. This is our destiny: to rid the earth of all those capable of destructive magic.* However, Marie knew he wouldn't stop at users of dark magic alone. No, he would kill any and all witches if he could. He felt it was their birthright.

Marie felt differently.

She wanted to find a way to coexist. She had friends who were witches, and her mother had found peace among them before she died. Marie chose to follow in her mother's footsteps. Plus, she wouldn't have Judson if she went along with the idea of who they thought a witch hunter should be. Judson may not have been a witch, but he was raised by one within an entire coven of witches. So to Dante, Judson was just as evil.

Marie paused in front of an open window and gazed out at their beautiful new surroundings they called home—well, not so new, considering they had been living in the quaint box canyon area for a few years now. The sight of the mountains boxing them in on all four sides still warmed her heart and freely offered her peace, especially when a fresh thin layer of snow had fallen overnight, as it had the past night. Snow was early for September but not unheard of in the mountains. It wouldn't last through the day, however. The sun had just barely begun to make its ascent into the sky, but soft pink still welcomed the coming day.

Marie smiled when she noticed man-sized footprints traveling away from their home toward the shed Judson had set up as a blacksmith's forge. He had earned quite the reputation for his metalwork around town, and he'd been attempting to catch up on orders he had yet to fulfill. She had no doubt that was where he'd been since before dawn, working his heart out. Judson's personal metalwork took a back seat while he worked on orders for the townspeople, early in the morning or late into the evening, to make ends meet.

Marie dressed for the cold winds of fall she was about to face and wrapped herself with a heavy shawl. Theirs was a modest home built right next to the land they had claimed for the vineyard they were cultivating with such love and devotion. The house had just enough rooms for the family who had traveled with them: Marie's human father Hank, her human brother Rodney, her young adult hunter cousins Caroline and Michael, as well as a few other cousins who never fully awakened into their hunter side. Also, Rachael Stronghold—Marie's best friend from the coven Judson was raised in—and Ahote Ahusaka traveled and lived with them. Rachael and Ahote were now married with an emerging toddler named Alo Stronghold Ahusaka, after Ahote's brother and Rachael's maiden name for her mother who died before they had arrived. Needless to say, they were living in tight quarters.

Marie dreamed of one day being able to add additional rooms—perhaps even additional little cabins—to their home not only for family but for visitors who came to the area. The view was magnificent, and she wanted to share the peace and comfort she had found there with others. Then when the vineyard was fully functional and they had enough workers to sustain it, Marie dreamed of a larger, grander home closer to the falls to live out her days with Judson, hopefully raising a family of their own.

For the last several years since arriving in town, the original settlers had begun calling the area Whisper Falls due to the way the falls had beckoned them, whispering into their souls, to come. And when they stood in the center of the little canyon, the falls sounded like a whisper, and so they had begun to build the town in that very spot. However, other names had been bandied about—many wanted to include *haven* in the name, since that was the purpose of the town—and there was still much discussion about it.

As she exited the warm and cozy home—thanks to one of the early risers' forethought to build a fire—she inhaled slow and deep, feeling the sharp sting of the bitterly cold air as it flooded her lungs, and smiled. Though jarring, the feeling reminded her she was alive. She loved fall in the little box canyon. It wasn't unheard of to find snow this early; still, she proceeded with caution as she made her way toward the forge. Marie carefully avoided patches of ice and areas of thicker frost. Loving the squeaking sound her boots made against the snow, Marie paused to listen for the whispers from the falls. This time of morning, the town was quiet and the rushing water could clearly be heard. She closed her eyes and could practically feel the mist spray off the water and onto her face. Such a great sense of importance, of magic, and of purpose she felt next to the waters.

The memory instantly took her back to when they had first arrived. She and Judson had picnicked by the edge of the lower pool. She had just discovered that the stone set into the dagger Judson had given her had immense power when it touched the magical waters, but when it was interlocked with her ancestor's journal, the pages within had revealed much more about who she was as a Blackstone than she had ever known. The secrets and knowledge she had been seeking since her mother died had finally been revealed. It was also then and in that space, Judson Carter proposed to her—again. His action was not necessary, as they had been married in secret back in Virginia before they left, but he wanted to make a symbolic statement of their new life.

Shortly after they established their life in the mountains and secured their position, they had asked Raffaele Augustine to marry them again. She wanted friends, not just strangers, to witness their union. And it had taken them some time and experience to gain that trust and companionship she had so longed for.

# CHAPTER 2

*A*s Marie approached the shed, she could hear the clanging sounds of iron slamming against metal. She snuck into the forge, attempting not to disturb Judson while he worked with hot metal. Just as she was about to make her presence known, she watched Judson shake out his hand after the last hit with his hammer, only to realize extra sparks ascended into the air. Sparks not from the metal or the hot coals. Surprised confusion lit up his face. Marie cocked her head, wondering what could have caused the sparks, when she considered that perhaps he'd been working on her dagger. Since being infused with the water from the falls, the stone had lit with magic; the sparks could have come from that.

"Judson," she called out from around the wall to announce her entrance. Glancing at him, she saw him quickly put his hand behind his back before he reached for his hammer once more. "Everything all right in here?" she asked.

Moving around to the front of the fire, he briefly frowned, then smiled at her. "You're up early. Everything fine at the house?"

She noticed he didn't answer her question.

"I woke up from a disturbing dream where you disappeared from me again, so I came to check on you."

He came to her and placed his free hand upon her shoulder. His warm brown eyes bored into her soul. "I'm right here, Marie. I don't like you having these recurring nightmares. Sure you're all right?"

She nodded, though the memory of the dream made her shudder. "I know it was just a dream, but I needed to see you awake."

Judson watched her for a moment more before he returned to the fire and picked up his hammer. Judson was tall and muscular. His dark blond hair had grown longer and appeared dirtier than normal, working amidst all the soot and smoke.

"I'm almost finished with the repair work on your dagger. I smoothed out the blade as well." He lifted the dagger that had been in her family for centuries to show her his work. Only in the last several years did she discover that the dagger had originally been in her family for many years—and the Stronghold coven had been keeping it safe—and because of her family's journal, she learned more of the dagger's properties and how it might have worked for her ancestors. Judson had been tinkering with it and found learning about the round stone fascinating. Before they arrived, the stone was colorless. Then Marie infused the smooth rock with a magical aether, turning it to a glowing blueish green, when she mixed the stone with the water from the falls. Inscribed on the blade itself was a Latin phrase: *Elige tibi.* Translated, it meant: Choose yourself.

And that was exactly what Marie had done in order to free what family she could and herself. She chose the kind of witch hunter she and her descendants would have the opportunity to be.

Marie moved around to the other side of the circular stone fire pit containing a raging fire in order to watch Judson put the finishing touches on her dagger before dipping it in the cool water to solidify his work. His actions were smooth and graceful, practiced and perfect for working on even the most delicate piece of metal. Marie's eyes never left him. She watched each movement, evaluating him. Something was wrong, though, and he hadn't shared it with her—and that bothered her the most.

"Jud? Are *you* all right? You seem a little off," she said casually, watching his reaction, waiting for his reply.

He slowed his swing but didn't fully stop. "I woke up a little shaky, but I'm sure it'll wear off. Perhaps I'm just hungry. I didn't eat before coming out this morning. I didn't want to wake you."

"Oh, Judson, you know you need to eat before expending all that energy. I'll go fix you something right now and bring it back." Of course, that had to have been all it was. He burned so many calories and so much energy when he worked in the forge. "I'll see if Rachael and Ahote are up, and we'll all come out for breakfast." Marie headed back the way she entered but looked over her shoulder at him before she left.

"Sounds great, love. I'm famished. But I'll be in shortly—no reason to have them all traipse out here in the cold of the morning." Judson wiped the sweat from his brow, causing the hair to stick up at the top of his head, then he winked at her.

The wind picked up as soon as she left the outbuilding. Marie clenched her wrap tightly around her shoulders, ducked her chin, and dashed back to the house. Upon entering, she heard all the voices joyously chatting in the kitchen. She loved how they all still wanted to live together, but someday soon they would definitely need more room. Marie chuckled to herself and smiled at the heavenly sounds of grease popping on the griddle, eggs cracking in a bowl, and the fire crackling, accompanied by the most delicious smells. Breakfast was already underway.

"Everything smells so good in here!" Marie walked into the kitchen, inhaling with a smile the entire way. "I hope I didn't wake you," she said, putting her arms around Rachael, who stood in front of the cast-iron wood stove, checking the sizzling bacon.

She and Rachael Stronghold had been friends forever. When

Marie needed to leave her home and family in Virginia to head out west with a traveling wagon train to get away from her crazed witch hunter brother, Dante, Rachael and some others from their coven chose to join her—plus Dante and his group had pretty much destroyed the Strongholds' entire village, and they had nowhere else to go. Still, Rachael had been Marie's biggest supporter since her mother, Cessily, had died. Since moving out west, Marie wanted to support Rachael in return.

Rachael's mom had died during the raid Dante and his band had inflicted upon their coven. Marie owed Rachael a life debt—at least that was how Marie saw it. And now, Rachael and Ahote's first child was a part of their family. Marie couldn't contain her excitement. She considered all of them under her protection within the new town, and as such, she claimed them as her family—as Blackstones.

Rachael had prematurely gained the leadership of the Stronghold coven at the death of her mother. Since arriving, Rachael had offered her people—those who had remained with them—the opportunity to join the Luna coven while she studied and grew in her own powers and magic.

"Not at all. In fact, I was waiting for you to get up. When I heard you moving around, I got up, but you had already walked outside. Will Judson be joining us?" She smiled and picked up a slice of bacon with a fork and flipped it over.

"Yes, he'll be along shortly. And he's famished, so I'll make some more," Marie said with a laugh.

Rachael turned to look at Marie, cocked her head, and frowned. "What's wrong?"

Marie dropped her arms and took a step back, looking intently at her friend. "How do you do that?"

"What?"

"That thing where you always know something is either wrong or about to go wrong," Marie added, knowing full well Rachael knew exactly what she was talking about.

She shrugged. "I don't know what you mean."

"Of course you don't. It's part of your witchy heritage, and you don't listen to it enough, if I'm honest about it."

"So . . . what is it?"

Marie sighed and looked around the room to see everyone busy with either setting the table, cooking something else, or reading. "I had another dream last night."

"About Judson?"

"Yes . . . and no. It was strange. There was more to it this time, more involvement with the town and something dark creeping in. I couldn't find Judson, and then he jumped in front of me with my dagger shooting light from it, defending me. And a strange voice was calling to be released—for me to release them. At first I thought it was Judson, but then it changed. I didn't recognize it. I think it was a woman, but I couldn't be sure."

Rachael frowned. "I don't like it. Something is going on."

"You don't think it's pre-party nervous dreams?" Marie tried to lighten the moment. Rachael smirked, knowing what she intended.

"Oh no!" Rachael cried, realizing she had let a piece of bread burn. She quickly attempted to put out the small flame and save the toast. But Ahote was immediately at her side, pushing her out of danger and smothering the fire out of the now smoking piece of bread.

Just then Judson came in and burst into laughter. "I leave you for just a little while and you practically burn down the new house," he said with good humor.

"Ha ha, very funny," Rachael threw back at him.

Judson playfully patted Rachael on the shoulder with brotherly affection, then went to see if he could assist Ahote. "You have it under control?"

"Yes." Ahote nodded. "I will go to work with the grapes today, right Atsidi?" Atsidi was a name Ahote and his brothers had called Judson from the beginning. It was a word that meant

11

*blacksmith* in their native language and became a term of endearment for him.

"Yes. Rodney goes with you today, and I will be along this afternoon," Judson replied, turning to Rodney to ensure that was his plan as well.

"I'm heading there after we eat." Rodney nodded, tipping his head back down to what was left of his coffee. "We have a public opening to get that wine ready for!"

"Then we have a plan for today," Judson said, taking a vigorous bite off the end of a piece of bacon straight out of the pan and ending with a big cheesy grin.

# CHAPTER 3

*L*ater that day, Marie, Rachael, and little Alo took a slow leisurely walk into the main part of town. The air still held the crisp edge of the beginning of fall, but the sun was out, and the combined mix of warm and cold was a refreshing combination.

"What is on your list for today?" Rachael asked, helping little Alo with dark hair and skin like his father, but with green eyes like his mother.

"I am headed to meet the Trents, Gregory and Charlotte, to commission them to make something for Judson as a gift. They make the most beautiful music boxes and timepieces."

"Oh, what a wonderful idea!" Rachael gushed.

Marie's gaze took in all the new growth in the town. Since they had arrived only a handful of years ago, more buildings had gone up around what was being referred to as the town square. Most of the dirt roads still remained except for the ones they had paved with cobblestones like they saw done in the bigger cities, and more efforts had been made to cultivate greenery and decoration as well. And more homes had been built for those who decided to remain and make the beautiful box canyon their home. Several more families had joined them since they settled, and of those, only a few of the families were additional witches. The original group who had traveled with them across the country were considered the elders—or founding families. They gathered together and held meetings on the regular to discuss town issues, the most recent of which had been how many non-supernaturals, or non-magical, people had moved in and how best to keep their secrets to ensure the safety of all.

"I can't believe how much has changed since we first arrived here," Rachael said, gazing around at the new growth.

"It's not only the town that is growing, but the families are as well." Marie's voice took on a wistful tone as she glanced lovingly at Rachael and Ahote's son of three. They had him shortly after they had gotten settled and married just after arriving. Marie couldn't be happier for her friend.

"Speaking of . . ." Rachael raised her eyebrows in silent question to Marie, who couldn't help the blush that crept up her neck.

"Soon. I don't know how soon, yet, but we would like to start our family now we are settled. I just feel like it's not the right time yet."

Rachael nodded. "Honor your intuition, Marie. You'll know when it's right, no matter how much I want to see you with a little one of your own." She smiled and looped her arm through Marie's just like old times, but reached for her son's hand, uniting them in the new times.

"How is Ahote adjusting?" Marie asked, knowing it had been hard with the loss of his brother, Alo, and then even harder when the other, Cetanwakuwa, left town for his own pursuits. They had never been separated since they'd been born. Then during their travels, they were attacked by Dante and his group of rogue witch hunters. The band of travelers Marie and her family traveled with included many strong witches, more than one frost dragon shifter, several members of the fae community, and other supernaturals. She was proud to be a part of their group, and even had hoped to find friendship amongst them.

Along their journey, they met the three Ahusaka brothers—men native to the lands they traveled through and gifted in their own rights. Ahusaka, they learned, meant *wings* and was fitting, as they were hawk shifters. Alo, the eldest, had fallen during the fight with Dante. His name meant *spiritual guide*, and he was the shaman and wise man of the three. Cetanwakuwa, the middle brother's name, meant *attacking hawk*, and he was the fighter. But Ahote—*restless one*, the youngest of the three—had fallen in love with Marie's best friend in the whole world.

"He's adjusting, I think. It's all very different for him to be in a structured environment and a father on top of all of it, especially without his brothers, whom he has always had around. It's been a challenge for him. But he's handling it for now. Though, as his name signifies, I sense a restlessness within him. He's like a wild animal, content and used to freely roaming the world. I know he loves me, but sometimes I'm concerned I'm keeping him here against his nature."

Marie could also see the restlessness stirring underneath Ahote's skin, but he seemed to tame it with his growing love for Rachael and their son. Marie gripped her friend's hand. "I'm always here for you. But he seems happy. He lights up whenever you or Alo enter the room."

"That little boy is his world." Rachael smiled, looking down at the child with his bright green eyes and dark curly hair. Alo looked up at her with pure adoration before jumping in a puddle from melted snow, splashing his mom with a giggle. Rachael exasperatedly looked to Marie. "Now, where do we find the tinkers?"

Marie pointed off in the direction of where the Trents' home shop was. "It's not far now. I'm excited to see if they can build what I am envisioning for Judson." Marie beamed from ear to ear, lost in her own imagination.

"Well, let's ask them. I see Charlotte entering their shop now," Rachael said, lifting her hand in a wave toward Charlotte Trent. The Trents' store was a brick facade lined with rich lumber adorned with a sign that read, *Horologist: Timepieces, Music Boxes & Gifts.*

"Hello, Charlotte," Marie called, also waving, causing Charlotte to turn and see them coming toward her.

Charlotte smiled, waved, and beckoned them to enter the shop. In her late fifties, she looked bright and full of energy. She wore her customary leather apron with pockets for her tools. Marie didn't know Charlotte or her husband Gregory well, as they hadn't been in town long, but she admired their talent with woodworking and level of expertise with their detailed timepieces. They also had done a magnificent job with the repairs on the Whisper Falls Inn's conservatory.

"Hello, ladies, won't you come inside?" said the Trents' apprentice, who also helped run the shop. Behind them, the heavy door decorated with intricate carvings and patterns Marie didn't recognize closed, followed by the welcoming sound of chimes. "What brings you to our little shop on such a lovely day?" Theodore Carver asked, as Charlotte smiled and played for a moment with little Alo in Rachael's arms before she went back to work on a project. In his late twenties, Theodore was the Trents' assistant and took orders for them as well.

"I have an idea I'm hoping to commission you and the Trents to make for me to give my Judson as a gift to celebrate the opening of the vineyard," Marie explained.

"I see. Well, that sounds wonderful. Won't you give me some more information on what you're dreaming up? If you could draw something for me, that would be most helpful as well. Gregory is not in the shop at the moment, but I'll include him in the process when he returns."

"Thank you, Theodore!" Marie clapped her hands in excitement. "This is going to be magical!" She winked at Rachael, who practically rolled her eyes at Marie's lack of subtlety. They followed him inside to the workshop and stood around a worktable, half of which was a chaotic mess filled with papers, screws, springs, and other oddities. The other half was clean, with everything in its place, and contained a stack of small boxes and trays of tiny parts.

"How's Betsy?" Marie asked. She was excited to see him beginning to settle down with the lovely young woman.

"She's well, thank you." Theodore smiled at her, then fiddled with some levers and pulls, and the table unfolded to a larger workspace. He then pulled out a piece of blank paper and handed a writing utensil to Marie.

"Marie, I should have asked, but what kind of item are you hoping we can create for you?" Theodore asked.

"A box. Similar to the famed puzzle boxes the Trents make, but a little less puzzle and a little bigger box. I'm thinking maybe something he could put some of his prized daggers or delicate metal creations inside."

Theodore nodded as if he completely understood what Marie wanted. "Could you draw the basic shape and size, or any defining characteristics you are looking for?"

Marie took the pencil and for a moment sketched some of her thoughts onto paper. "I'm not the most practiced artist, but I think this is the basic idea." She stood back and allowed Theodore to look at her drawing while she noted Rachael following Alo as he toddled around the room—trying to keep his hands out of all that looked dangerous or breakable in the space, which seemed to be a feat in itself. Marie smiled. Rachael and her son were endearingly comical to watch.

"This is doable," Theodore finally said matter-of-factly. He asked Marie a few more clarifying questions about the detail work and how many puzzle pieces she wanted. They discussed payment and all the final details, then it was time to go.

"Oh, Marie, when do you want this finished?" Theodore asked as he wrote down a few notes.

"By the opening a month from now. Which you, Betsy, Charlotte, and Gregory are, of course, invited to. I have yet to get the invitations out," Marie sheepishly explained.

"Consider it done."

"Thank you, Theodore. I can't wait to see it!" Marie and Rachael said their goodbyes to Theodore and waved at Charlotte, not wanting to disturb her while she worked, then left with the sound of the chimes echoing behind them.

Marie, Rachael, and little Alo walked through town a bit longer, then headed home before the afternoon grew too chilled for the little one to be out.

# CHAPTER 4

$\mathcal{T}$he Court of the Sun and the Moon was the leadership of the town. The Court consisted of a representative from each of the founding families who had arrived in 1854 as part of the wagon train. The Blackstone witch hunters had always been a matriarchy, so Marie was the seat holder to attend all the meetings about the goings on of the town. Currently, they met in a home near a small park close to the entrance into the town. The home was a beautiful mansion belonging to Elsmed Fairchild and his wife, and all the members comfortably gathered in.

The Court was an eclectic mix of supernaturals—and one human—including witches, mages, moroi—which Marie had learned was a type of vampire—fae, wolf shifters, a frost dragon, and others.

"Find your seat," Anne-Marie Beaumont announced, getting everyone's attention. "Let us begin tonight. We have much to discuss." Anne-Marie was one of the leaders of the Luna Coven, along with Raffaele Augustine and Rodavan Bishop, and as such, also acted as one of the leaders of the Court as she brought them all together, revealing the need for a body of leadership to govern their small but growing town.

Marie had an uneasy feeling. She paid attention to Anne-Marie's expression while she watched everyone find their seats. Something was wrong.

"Friends, tonight we have to discuss an urgent matter that has recently come to my attention. Witches have been disappearing from our town—young witches, from those not much older than my Saundra up to those their early twenties."

A collective gasp came from everyone in the room.

"Are you sure? What if they are simply leaving?" Lawrence Mills, the frost dragon, suspiciously asked with his deep smooth voice, though by the looks on faces, everyone wondered the same.

"Family members have come forward saying their loved ones have simply vanished. No word. No mention of leaving. Just there one moment and gone the next. I can feel it in my being— the threads of the witches within my coven are no longer there. Not barely noticeable as if out of town or reach . . . simply gone," Anne-Marie explained, wringing her hands together with apparent worry.

"That is troubling indeed," Raffaele Augustine concurred.

Rodavan Bishop sat quietly to Anne-Marie's right with no expression, but looked into the eyes of everyone present until landing on Marie's, where he paused. Marie felt him, as if he attempted to seek answers from her very being. If she had any, she would gladly give them up. He then continued his perusal around the room. Marie felt affronted, as if he thought she had something to do with the disappearances.

"Does anyone have any information that could be useful?" Anne-Marie asked hopefully. "Anything strange you've noticed around town? Anything we could piece together to make sense of any of this?"

People shook their heads with nothing to offer.

"I don't think this really has anything to do with it, but I'll share just in case . . ." Marie took a deep breath. "I've had dreams of late. Dreams of issues I believe are personal, but there are moments in the dreams where the town is involved, and a darkness lurks at the edges of town and creeps closer until it morphs into the people, turning them into smoky shapes with dark tendrils." She paused to look around, and as she expected, everyone present simply stared at her, unsure what to say.

"That is definitely interesting, Marie," Anne-Marie finally said with a frown. "Far be it from me to judge how and where potential information comes from. Especially as we are supernatural beings who deal with magic and the unexpected every day. Thank you for sharing. We will continue to take it into account with all other information we gather."

Marie nodded, appreciating Anne-Marie's words. Suddenly she could feel a tension brewing in the room, a dissension stirring in the air. Some of the members openly stared at her. She even heard a few murmuring under their breaths to their neighbors. Her eyes shot toward Lawrence Mills specifically as he grumbled to Elsmed Fairchild sitting next to him. She knew Lawrence never truly liked her, and she didn't care, but to be so open about it in one of their meetings was going too far. Anger rose in Marie's chest. She had put her life on the line to save these people on the long journey they had taken together. She had fought against her own brother to stand among these people, to side with them and their beliefs for a better future side by side. How dare they!

Marie stood to her feet and shot her gaze directly at Lawrence. "I'm happy to undergo a test by Elsmed if you have a problem with me."

Lawrence raised his hands to placate her, but Rodavan unexpectedly rose. "I do not think that is necessary at this point, Marie. We all know what you have put on the line for this town, and we respect it. Do not underestimate that we will take into consideration *any* and *all* information that comes forward, no matter whom it refers to, but for now we are simply discussing it."

Marie frowned. He wasn't really standing up for her. He was

simply putting aside what he believed could be the inevitable at some point. She huffed but nodded and sat back down. Perhaps she had been defensive and jumped to conclusions.

"I do not believe there is any involvement from Marie or any of the Blackstone hunters," Anne-Marie confidently stated. "But this is a very serious issue, and we need to all be watching and keeping an eye out for anything unusual in the town. We cannot allow any more witches—or anyone for that matter—to disappear. It simply seems the witches are being targeted for some unknown reason."

"We will be most diligent in our efforts," Gaby Kasun acknowledged with sincerity. She then offered Marie a slight nod and a small smile. Marie didn't know Gaby well, but she had been around since they first arrived. Rumor had it Gaby and the Kasun Pack had been around long before the wagon train arrived, keeping watch over the forest and the sleeping box canyon, waiting for the next inhabitants. Marie heard stories about a tribe who lived there long before their arrival in 1854, leaving the Kasuns and a mysterious presence to watch over and protect the area.

"Thank you, Gaby," Anne-Marie said.

"We will as well. There have been some new travelers stopping by the inn. We'll keep our eyes and ears open," Mihail Petran said in his thick Romanian accent. He and his wife opened Whisper Falls Inn at the corner of the town square. Anyone new in town would most likely visit their inn first.

"I expect nothing less from everyone. For now, be dismissed. Thank you, Elsmed, for the use of your home. We will meet here again next week. And thank you all for coming," Anne-Marie concluded.

Everyone stood to leave without so much as an exchange of pleasantries. Conversations and interactions were limited; the topic at hand seemed to weigh heavily upon all present.

As Marie gathered her leather satchel and placed it over her head and across her chest, she felt a hand on her elbow, then turned.

"I want you to know, I believe you, Marie. You have no reason to think we doubt you. Some here might, but they doubt themselves, too. I wouldn't let it bother you. But that said, if anything happens or anyone comes against you, please inform me, and I'll get involved." Anne-Marie offered her a warm smile of assurance and confidence.

"Thank you; that means a lot." And it did. Marie stood taller, more confident she was believed. She wanted nothing more than to fit in with the town and be a part of it, ensuring her legacy became an integral part of the town in the years to come. Being a witch hunter who didn't hunt witches would wear down her physical being at some point. She would still live an unusually long life, but not as long as Dante would. Marie wanted the future set for the descendants she hoped to have.

But for now, she pondered what could possibly be happening to their town as she bundled up for her chilly walk home, only to find Judson waiting for her outside. Sitting up in the horse-drawn buggy, he was wrapped with a warm blanket, wearing an even warmer smile upon his face as she ran toward him.

"I thought we could go for an evening ride," Judson said, throwing part of the blanket over Marie's lap.

"I would love that, thank you." She leaned up and kissed his cheek as he led the horse back onto the lamp-lit street.

# CHAPTER 5

*J*udson pulled the horse and buggy up to a hitching post at the base of the trail to the great and mighty falls. The settling families had decided something magical resided within the water.

"It's such a beautiful but chilly night," Marie said, wrapping a wool shawl around her shoulders. Their visible breaths floated into the evening air, practically crystallizing as they spoke.

"It is," Judson agreed, as he finished tying the horse's lead to the post. "I wanted to come out and enjoy it with you." He smiled, but it didn't quite reach his eyes.

Marie frowned and raised an eyebrow. She knew him too well and for too long to think that tonight there was no more than him simply picking her up on a whim.

"Fine." He sighed. "I got wind of the topic of tonight's meeting from Anne-Marie beforehand. She was afraid some of the members might get ruffled up and wanted me in place. Just in case." He shrugged his shoulders as if there was nothing to it. "Is everything all right?"

Marie laced her hand through his. "Let's walk to our spot at the falls." She referred to the place where he proposed when they had first arrived. It happened to also be the place she discovered more of her witch hunter heritage when her family's journal revealed its hidden secrets. "There are some who doubt my sincerity . . . or possibly my trustworthiness, in the town. But I'm determined to prove them wrong and solidify my place among the townspeople and among the leaders of it."

Judson sharply nodded with a smirk. "I knew you'd bounce back just fine."

He removed his hand from hers and wrapped his arm around her shoulders as they continued their walk along the barely worn path, leading them to their spot by the small lake at the base of the falls.

Marie felt Judson hesitate when they neared the waters. She cocked her head and tried to pay attention to every small nuance of her husband. He had never reacted like that at the water's edge before—almost as if he was unnerved by it. She stopped them and turned Judson to face her, holding both his hands.

"Judson, something is bothering you. What is it?"

His expression shut down, hiding any indication that something was indeed wrong. He cleared his throat and looked out beyond her at the water. "It's really nothing, Marie. I think I've just been too immersed in working on your dagger and the stone within it—trying to understand how it truly works with the journal, what we can learn from it, and how we might best use it for our benefit. I know for certain it has magical properties, but what it can do, I have yet to ascertain."

Marie wondered if she was reading too much into his responses. Perhaps he was simply exhausted and overworked. She was about to tell him how he needed to take more breaks and ask if she could participate the next time he worked on her dagger, but she paused and whipped her head to the side. She then clutched her stomach and quietly moaned.

"There's a presence of black magic, but it's vague," she whispered.

Judson grabbed her and held her close, but Marie wriggled out of his full hold to have a hand free in case she needed to fight. As quickly as the feeling came, it left, leaving Marie more relaxed. She inhaled deeply, held it for a moment, then exhaled slowly. "It's gone."

Judson, too, relaxed minutely, though not yet sure the danger was gone.

"That was odd. Wait. Someone's nearby. I feel them watching us, but it's different than the black magic." Marie again spoke in hushed tones, so as not to be heard by any but Judson.

"I feel someone's presence too." Judson followed her gaze, then continued to look in the other direction.

They were interrupted by a sound of something rustling in the bushes a short distance behind them and away from the falls. The sounds grew louder and louder until a couple of shadows became visible in the night.

"No need for alarm, you two," a man's voice came from the shrubs as he made his way into a patch of light. Ric Kasun emerged, followed by his wife and alpha, Gaby Kasun.

"Forgive us; we did not intend to startle you," said Gaby.

"You did, but only for a moment." Judson smiled and relaxed.

"Just before you showed up, I felt something. I think it was black magic," Marie shared with a concerned expression. "But then it just disappeared, as if not there at all."

The Kasuns both nodded.

"We didn't know what we were dealing with, but we received a lead regarding something or someone sneaking through the forest right after Gaby left the meeting," Ric explained.

"So we set out to track them. I caution you to be careful and perhaps not linger too long in secluded places at night, at least until the threat is found," Gaby warned.

"Thank you, but how can we help?" Marie asked. Judson nodded his agreement as he reached for her hand.

Gaby sympathetically smiled but shook her head. "Thank you for your offer, but we are simply doing a tracking exercise tonight to see if we can find any information or leads. So far, we don't have much to go on. But thanks to you, we know we might be dealing with a witch practitioner of black magic."

"Why would a witch be taking—or worse—other witches?" Marie asked with a deep frown.

Gaby looked to Ric, and they both shrugged. "We're not sure, but we'll keep the Court apprised of anything more we find, so you'll also be informed."

Marie nodded, knowing there wasn't anything the Kasuns could allow her to help with at the present time. Perhaps if they got more information, she could be of some help. "Good luck. I hope you find something to go on."

Ric and Gaby nodded their thanks and melded back into the shadows of the shrubbery and the darkness of the night. Marie couldn't help but wonder if they had changed from, and back into, their wolves, or if they tracked as humans.

# CHAPTER 6

*O*nce back home, Marie took Judson aside before they entered the large main room where they could hear the others still up visiting with each other.

"Jud, can I see the dagger and the stone? I know you've been working on it, but I want to see how it's coming along," Marie said in a hushed tone.

Judson grabbed her hand and led her to the secret bookcase that slid sideways with the pulling out of a specific book. Before the rest of the house was finished, Judson and Marie's father, Hank, and her brother Rodney worked long and hard hours creating a secret basement. The basement was filled with various weapons Judson had created. They began stockpiling, just in case the town came upon a time when they needed a vast amount of weapons. Also in the basement was a large, long table made of a slab of metal placed upon stabilizing wooden legs. Judson had laid out several different weapons and a couple of books open with sloppy writing scrawled across the paper and various rough drawings.

"What have you been doing? It looks like you're conducting experiments," Marie noted as she ran her hand across the metal top and along some of the journals.

Judson lowered his head. "I am. I didn't want to tell you until I had something more concrete to go on."

Marie frowned. "I could help. Why didn't you tell me?"

"I was so close to figuring something out. It started as a surprise, then it became an obsession."

"So explain what you're doing."

"I think the stone in your dagger, coupled with the aether in the water from the falls, will infuse metals with magical properties," Judson started to explain. "The metal speaks to me. Your dagger gave me the inspiration when I held it, and it showed me how to use magic to reproduce it."

"Okaaaay," Marie held out the word as she tried to understand where he was going with his line of thought.

"Don't you see? If we can infuse the metals with magic, the weapons we create could be designed to fight specific species or be used against certain kinds of magic, whereas a regular sword might fail."

"Oh . . ." She paused, understanding dawning upon her mind. "Oh! That's amazing, Judson! However did you realize this?" She grabbed one of the journals and leafed through Judson's scribblings, taking it all in.

"When I was tinkering with your dagger and the stone, I added some more of the water and was able to dissect the smallest portion—"

"You destroyed the stone?" Marie's eyes widened in horror, and she watched him retract his words.

"No, it's amazing! I sliced off the smallest bit using a magnifying glass and then it regenerated itself. It regenerated itself! I've never seen that. I think I've discovered some elements involved that make this a renewable source for the making of weapons. I'm not an alchemist, so I don't understand what everything I've discovered is, but I think we could talk to someone if you want. I think it should stay within the family for now, however. At least, until we know more . . ." Judson trailed off, realizing he had gone off topic.

"Wow, I don't even know what to say. This is what they meant in the journal, though! My journal is in the safety box in the wall. Can you hand it to me?" she asked, her eyes glossing over with thoughts of the possibilities. Judson handed her the journal, and Marie began to thumb through it, but then looked up and smiled. "I forgot. I need the stone to connect with it to make the hidden parts come forth. Such a brilliant maneuver by the witch who helped my family to create it."

"Agreed," Judson said with a smile. He reached for the dagger and gently placed the hilt in Marie's hand.

She examined the stone set within the delicate metalwork, and sure enough, the stone was complete and whole, not a scratch on it. Amazing. Marie positioned the journal just beneath the dagger. The metalwork on the cover was in the complete reverse from the design on the dagger, each resembling the shape of an elaborate butterfly, but truly it was the stars that made up the mark only witch hunters were born with. Both sides of the metalwork fit nicely together, like puzzle pieces locking into place. And when the lock clicked, Judson carefully placed a dropper of aether water on the stone, and it began to glow.

This time, however, Marie noted that Judson pulled his hand back extremely fast, trying his best not to get any of the water on his skin. But a drop of the water did land on his skin, and a spark flew out from his hand.

"Judson! What is happening to you?" Marie shouted.

"I . . . I don't know. I didn't want to scare you. I think it's something to do with the magic in the water. It's reactive on my skin. I've been trying not to touch it." Judson's face had gone pale, and an element of fear passed across his eyes.

"Scare me? Are you kidding? Do you know who we are and who our families are?" She laughed. "That's an absurd thought. But I can appreciate that you were unnerved by it and wanted to understand it for yourself before telling me." She frowned but continued with understanding. "It sounds like something I would have done to you."

"You're not mad?"

"Why would I be mad?" She pushed away his worries with a flick of her hand. "We'll figure this out together. But no more secrets, okay?"

"Agreed." Judson had the audacity to look sheepish before his next confession. "I have one more secret, but you can't know until the vineyard party. I'm sorry."

She laughed. "Fair enough. I have one of my own in that regard as well."

Marie winked at him, then examined his hand within her own. But what she felt was more than she had expected. Perhaps the aether in the water did more than simply react to his skin. She frowned but would have to see how it played out. For now, they needed to understand the great mystery of the magic-infused stone.

"Oh, look at this bit." Marie's words filled with fearful anticipation. "Of course, the first page I land on to read mentions the hunter's ability to suck out the magical souls of a witch once they are dead. That's creepy and definitely not what will win me points with the Court." She skipped a few more pages to see what else she might land on. "I wonder if there is anything in this about why my senses seem to be coming and going at random times." Her eyes scanned the pages furiously. "The Court is going to find this weapon information fascinating," Marie redirected their conversation to get them back on track. "The possibilities are endless."

"True. It also means we have within our midst a powerful artifact that, in the wrong hands, could be used against us or the town. So for now, we need to be careful with our information."

Marie nodded and ran her hand up to Judson's shoulder, where she rested it while they continued to examine the evidence before them. Judson told her of all his experiments and the outcomes he discovered.

"The truth in the outcome can't be completely verified unless used on a particular species, but there might be ways to test it in a minute manner without hurting anyone," Judson explained.

"I can't wait to hear how that's going to go over," Marie laughed.

# CHAPTER 7

The next day, Marie, Rachael, and—upon Judson's insistence for backup—Ahote traveled into the square with little Alo to get some sweets.

"Oh, Marie! Rachael!" a woman called from behind them. When Marie turned, she was pleasantly surprised to see Priscilla Augustine approaching her. Priscilla and her husband, Raffaele, as well as some of her husband's family, traveled among them on the wagon train, and Marie became quite fond of her over the time. Priscilla was young, in her early thirties, and a spitfire of a witch. Raffaele was a strong and powerful witch and sat on the Court with Marie.

"Hello, Priscilla!"

"Good afternoon, Priscilla," Rachael added as she handed Alo into Ahote's arms. "We were coming into town for a well-deserved treat. How is your day?"

"Very well, thank you, Rachael." Priscilla smiled at the little guy and tickled his hand as he reached out to touch their new visitor. "Marie, Raffaele shared your dream with me. I want you to know I find it very interesting. I believe in the power dreams have. It's a message . . . a warning even, for us. Could you please keep me apprised of any new developments? I'd like to try to help you sort through it if possible. Powerful dreams, along with the essence of a seer, run in my family, and I have a significant amount of experience with them."

Marie was a bit shocked Priscilla was being so forward about such things, but she glanced quickly around and found no one close enough to hear them.

"Thank you, Priscilla. It means the world to me you are taking it seriously. I'm sure most in that room last night did not." She put her hands on her waist in a subtle show of annoyance.

"Actually, I think you'd find more of them took it to heart than they let on. In our world, dreams can be significant portents of things to come," Priscilla explained with an air of gravity.

"Dreams are very important in my family also," Ahote said, surprisingly. He was often quiet when other people were around. But Marie knew he had found ease with Priscilla and her husband during their travels. "We must heed the warnings, but it is difficult when we do not yet understand them."

"Very true point, Ahote," Priscilla agreed. "So we must try to understand the best we can."

"I'll keep you informed if anything new should present itself to me," Marie said, acutely aware that several people had slowed down near them. Not close enough to listen, but close enough that it was unmistakable who they were watching. She felt a chill of unease slide up her back.

"I think it's time we get our treat and head home," Rachael said, also picking up on the attention they seemed to be drawing.

"Why are they staring at you like that, Marie?" Ahote asked quietly.

"Because they think I have something to do with the disappearances of late," Marie grimly replied. But then she got mad. Marie stood tall and faced the handful of people staring at her with a determined look on her face.

"Oh, Marie, this might not be the time," Priscilla warned under her breath. "I will stand with you, but you must be careful not to make a scene."

Marie gave her a curt nod. "I'll just go speak peacefully with them then."

She took two steps in the direction of the witches who stared at her as if she were guilty.

Before she could even open her mouth, a youngish girl—a witch—stumbled out from the alleyway between the buildings. Her hair was a matted mess, but everything else about her appearance was presentable, nothing torn or tattered. Her complexion, however, was pale and her face gaunt. Perhaps she hadn't been attacked. Perhaps this had nothing to do with the other witches. Perhaps . . .

"Help," she spoke with a gravelly tone, as if her words were raked across jagged rocks. She practically fell on top of Marie, who caught her before she hit the ground. Everyone gasped in surprise.

"Are you all right?" Marie asked in panic. "Who did this to you?" she rushed out, sensing the girl's wherewithal would expire soon.

"Vampire," she uttered before passing out.

"Did she say vampire?" Priscilla asked with a whisper, kneeling down to place her hand on the girl's forehead.

Marie nodded, unsure even what to say.

"Could that be?" Rachael asked, kneeling down on the opposite side and placing her hand on the girl's wrist. Both witches felt for the girl's life force.

Priscilla frowned and said, "I suppose anything is possible."

"Is she . . . ?" Ahote hedged his words, sensing the growing crowd.

"No, but her essence—you know the one of which I speak —is almost fully drained. She will never practice . . . or I should say, she'll never use those talents again." Priscilla shook her head in dismay, still fully aware that those beginning to surround them were not all supernatural members of the community.

Marie stood and addressed the crowd. "Someone go get the doctor! This girl has passed out from malnourishment. She needs medical attention right away."

Several people scattered to retrieve the necessary help.

"Good thing the doctor is a member of the coven," Priscilla whispered.

"Indeed." Marie held the limp girl in her arms and carefully looked over her face. "Not a scratch on her. But why is her hair in such disarray? She had to have fought off something. It doesn't make sense her attacker was a vampire if her blood is still intact."

"Energy parasite," Ahote supplied. "Like a vampire but steals energy. I have heard stories of such a thing long ago. A type of demon."

"An energy vampire?" Rachael's face scrunched up quizzically. Ahote nodded and watched those around them carefully as he held their son close in his arms.

Marie noted the fear in his eyes. "Ahote, why don't you take Rachael and Alo home. I'll wait to speak with Anne-Marie and then be shortly behind you."

A look of understanding passed between Marie and Ahote. Whoever was taking the witches most likely was draining them for their energy, and she didn't want Rachael or their little one in the line of fire, so to speak. And neither did he. About to protest, Rachael saw the look her husband gave her as he motioned toward their little one, which she, of course, could not argue with. Rachael would do anything to protect their young one.

Two women with long work dresses held up their hems, rushed up, and lowered themselves to the ground next to Marie. Anne-Marie Beaumont and another member of the Luna Coven performed their own quick assessments of the girl while Marie and Priscilla moved gently out from under the girl.

"Come, let's get her into the wagon the doctor brought," Anne-Marie directed, pointing to a horse-drawn wagon ready to go. Marie hadn't even heard the hooves or the wheels of the wagon pull up next to them in her focus on the girl. She barely even felt the girl's witch essence; hardly any remained in her system.

The doctor bent down and scooped the frail girl into his arms, careful not to jostle her too much. He then laid her in the flatbed of the wagon on top of a pile of blankets, and the witches climbed in after to surround her with love, protection, and whatever healing energy they could sustain her with until they took her away.

"Come, Marie and Priscilla," Anne-Marie called. "I need to know all you saw and anything she might have said."

Marie and Priscilla climbed up into the bench seat of the wagon next to the good doctor, followed by Anne-Marie. And as quickly as they arrived, they dashed away to Anne-Marie's home.

# CHAPTER 8

*I*nside the beautiful home, the witches laid the girl—in her late teenage years—on the dining room table and gathered around her. Marie stood back to give the witches room but also for herself, as her witch hunter senses tingled all up and down her arms almost to the point where it was too much to bear and she would need to leave the room. But thankfully, the witches chanted a few spells and then it was over. She relaxed for just a moment with the release of their power, but their presence alone still had a large effect on her being. Marie didn't recognize the girl, so she watched each of the women there to determine who her mother was.

"She is stable for now," one of the witches declared, "but I am afraid the part of her that makes her witch is now greatly diminished, to the point she may not be able to ever practice magic again."

A woman she recognized as a member of the Luna Coven, but whose name she didn't know, ran up to the girl, sobbing, and threw herself over the girl's chest. Marie instantly could see this was the girl's mother. It made her heart relieved to know the girl would feel her comfort.

"This is unacceptable," another woman spat. "Something

must be done to stop it." She had the audacity to turn and glare at Marie. She practically felt the force of the energy behind the witch's stare hit her, causing her to gasp.

"Now, just a minute." Priscilla physically stepped in front of Marie. "I was there. I saw the entire thing, and even if I hadn't been, Marie has no part in whatever is happening. She and her family have lived peacefully among us for these past several years, and we got to know them even before that. Her heart is good and pure."

Marie stepped up beside Priscilla, placing her hand on her arm, grateful to have a friend stand up for her and her family, but she was not willing to let someone else be her shield. She would stand up for herself as well. The tension in the room grew. Some deflated, hearing the truth in Priscilla's words, while the others needed someone to blame. Marie understood that.

Clearing her throat and redirecting the room, Anne-Marie asked, "Marie and Priscilla, could you share what transpired right before she collapsed?"

Marie nodded. "Of course. We were standing in front of the sweets shop talking with Priscilla, who had just joined us—us being Rachael, Ahote, their son, and myself—and we were about to find a treat for the little one. From the alley behind us, this girl"—Marie pointed toward the table—"stumbled out, barely conscious, with the look of death knocking on her door, and I caught her as she fell onto me."

"She had called for help just before she fell," Priscilla added, "and then Marie asked her who had done this to her, and she said 'vampire.' But upon our inspection of her, there were no puncture wounds and her blood flow seemed strong to me. Rachael and I both checked her witch essence, noting how drained she was, and that's when we called for someone to get the doctor and you." Priscilla nodded toward Anne-Marie.

"We discussed the possibility—along with Ahote, who concurred he had heard stories from his people of such a creature—of someone who could steal energy rather than blood.

So perhaps not an actual vampire. Just a thought we discussed," Marie offered.

"Very interesting indeed." Anne-Marie pursed her lips in deep thought as she glanced at each person in the room. "I'm not aware of any in town with the capacity to do such a thing. Could it be someone already here with a power they hid from us?"

No one had an answer for her.

"In my dreams, the waterfall calls to us. But not only us," Priscilla started to say in a wistful tone, almost a semi-trance state. Marie wondered if she was channeling her seer gift at that very moment. "Others will follow the path to the water. Others will be drawn by the power of the falls. Many will be invited to remain, and many we do not wish to stay." Priscilla shook her head, and her eyes cleared. She looked directly at Anne-Marie. "More needs to be done to strengthen the wards. This is a warning to us all."

Marie stared in awe at her friend. She had never seen her access that part of her witch gifts. Her skin felt the bumping effects of a chill that ran up her spine. But Priscilla was right. They needed stronger wards around the town.

"Is there still a possibility it could be a witch hunter? Unrelated, of course, Marie," a witch named Martha Daryn asked with a snide and accusatory tone.

Marie hadn't cared for her much before she spoke, now even less so. "No, it's not a witch hunter's power to siphon energy from a witch. Only when a witch hunter kills a witch do they absorb their magical essence as a life-sustaining substance . . . unless . . ." Marie paused, suddenly unsure. "Well, I suppose it could be possible if they had an outside power source assisting, but I've never heard of one."

For the first time since arriving in the small town, Marie felt like an outsider, like she didn't belong. By her own words, she fed the suspicion the doubters had already been nurturing. She thought of her family. Not only was it a tragedy and dangerous for the witches, but she hadn't thought of how it could turn to a danger for her own family.

"Thank you for your transparency, Marie," Anne-Marie said, sensing the sudden shift of tensions in the room. "You have always been such a support and a leader in guiding your family to merging into the community we have all built here together."

Marie could tell she was attempting to shine a positive light on the resident witch hunters, but she had her own doubts it would work.

"For now, our work here is done. The girl will recover, but sadly her magic will not. We will keep a twenty-four-hour watch on her along with her parents and hope when she wakes up she can tell us what happened and who did this to her. Until then, everyone return to your homes and your families. Keep everyone safe, keep your eyes open, be diligent, and no one go anywhere alone. Blessed be," Anne-Marie concluded with a bowed head.

"Blessed be," came the collective response.

"Blessed be," Marie said under her breath, unsure if she should say it with the rest of them or not. Marie ducked out of the home before anyone could speak to her. She needed to get home. She needed to think, and she needed to speak to Judson. The situation had become more dire than she had ever ventured to guess it could. Her family needed to be ready for anything.

# CHAPTER 9

*M*arie was very disturbed by the turn of events and the conversations brought up over the last couple of days. She went to bed after having a painfully honest discussion with her family about their options if the town turned against them. Disturbed as she was, she shouldn't have been surprised she was visited by another dream.

In her dream, Marie ran down the aisle of the vineyard once again, but this time the people disappeared one by one. She noted, however, the only ones disappearing were witches. And not only did they disappear, but they turned into shadowy shapes sucked out of their places and into the forest of dark trees behind them. As they added their mass to the darkness within the forest, it grew and grew, taking on a giant, towering humanoid shape looming over the town until it was shrouded in darkness except for the lightning striking all around it.

"Marie . . . Marie . . . Judson, wake up!" Marie vaguely heard Rachael's voice in the backdrop of her dream, but it was enough to pull her out of the despair she had begun to feel and wake her up.

"Ahote says there is evil outside. Get your weapons, and let's go!" Rachael said, with a hint of fear but also the slightest hint of the thrill of the chase. She wasn't one to give up easily or back down from a fight, and they'd had a few trying to get where they were presently.

Judson jumped up at her words, grabbing his bedside gun before even pulling on his trousers and boots. Marie, too, threw on a wrap and her boots, grabbed her dagger and a pistol from the vanity, and followed him out of the room. Her breath was uneasy, as she still recovered from her dream.

"You all right?" Judson quietly asked, sparing a quick glance back at her.

She waved him off. "Yes, yes, I'm fine. Just another dream is all. Mainly the same, but . . ." She trailed off.

"But what?"

"The darkness grew as it sucked away the witches until it covered the entire town," she said with a shake of her shoulders, as an icy chill spread down her spine.

"Well, that's not good," Judson stated plainly.

"No, Judson, it's not." She was sure he would have said more or asked more questions if they hadn't been so quickly awoken in the middle of the night.

They met up with Ahote, Rachael, Hank, and Rodney, each carrying guns, at the front door.

"Do we know what's out there?" questioned Rodney, wiping the sleep from his eyes and barely getting the front of his nightshirt tucked into his trousers.

"No. Ahote woke up and said he felt the evil. I felt something trying to tamper with the wards I placed around the house, but whoever it was wasn't able to cross them," Rachael proudly said.

"Possible evil wanting to send us to our untimely graves. Got it," Rodney sarcastically stated as he prepared his gun.

"Who is with Alo?" Marie asked, needing to know everyone was taken care of.

"Caroline and Michael are with him," Rachael assured her.

"Let's go before it's too late and whoever is out there is

gone," Judson harshly whispered. Marie knew he didn't mean anything by his tone; he was nervous for his family and his home in case the worst should happen.

They snuck out the front door with great caution, knowing they had several feet until they reached the boundary of the protective wards Rachael had set. Each with their weapons extended, they searched the property for any sign of disturbance, any sign of movement.

"I don't see anything. Marie, do you feel anything witchy or otherwise?" Rachael asked.

Marie took a moment and closed her eyes to send her power out into the darkness of the night. Breathing in slowly, she focused on the stillness of the night, the lack of sound from nocturnal critters, and simply reached out her senses and felt.

"It's there, but it's faint," she finally said, opening her eyes. "The feeling is confusing because I feel it stronger one second then less another second, as if it's fluctuating. Which is highly unusual, as far as I've experienced." Marie frowned. She peered into the back area of the home but didn't see anything.

"I feel it again! It's moving that direction," Marie abruptly said, pointing out behind their property heading into the vast expanse of land that led up the mountain. "Whoever it is, is now moving fast."

"Ahote, can you track it?" Judson quickly asked.

Ahote nodded, unabashedly dropped his clothes and weapons, shifted right on the spot into a large hawk, and took to the sky with no hesitation or words.

"I sure wish I could do that," Marie said wistfully. "Not the losing my clothes part, but the flying part." She snickered.

Rachael laughed. "You're afraid of heights. You'd be like a bird that flapped from one low tree branch to another, never taking to the skies."

Marie huffed. "Don't shatter my dreams. Maybe being a bird would take away that fear. You never know."

"Well, if the person wasn't already gone, you two would

definitely scare them away with your talking alone," Hank grumbled, putting his gun down.

"Sorry, Dad. I already felt them go . . ." Marie stopped mid-sentence with a realization. "Actually, I didn't feel them *go*. I felt them simply disappear. The feeling was there and then just gone. That's not how it works. Usually it trails off as the witch gets farther away. My senses really seem to be off lately." Marie flexed her hands, examining them as if she could see something wrong.

At that moment, Ahote came back, walking as a man, from around the other side of the house, shaking his head and buttoning his shirt. "It is most unusual, but I lost them."

"Ahote, if you don't mind my asking, how do you track?" Hank asked.

"I, too, can track dark magic, similar to Marie, but only when in my bird form, and it is not the same every time. It is an unusual gift to me." He picked up his weapons, then twisted his hands around the edge of the dagger he held between his hands.

Marie turned to go inside.

"Where are you going?" Rodney asked.

Concern etched across her face, Marie faced them all straight on. "I . . . I need a moment to myself to think this over."

Marie didn't return to her room, but instead went into the room they referred to as the library, which was truly just a small room with a fireplace and a hand-built wood bookshelf with a few of their mementos, trinkets, and books they brought with them from their homes back east and things they had gathered since. She stoked the fire and curled up on the floor in front of it with an additional blanket until the fire heated the room. A feeling she hadn't felt in quite some time crept into her mind and being. Doubt. Marie hadn't doubted her ability or her senses until the meeting last night, when others looked upon her with suspicion and distrust.

"Why now? Why are my abilities having trouble now? Is it because I don't actively hunt witches?" she asked herself aloud, ashamed to even have to think the thoughts, but there they were, right at the forefront of her mind. Marie struggled to wrap her mind around what could be going on in the town and what her place in it all was. Clearly she was involved somehow; she just wasn't sure what that reason could be.

Sighing, Marie fixed her gaze on the flames growing tall and fierce. The heat radiated outward to wash over her in wave after wave of warmth. Gradually she let down the last blanket she had piled on top of her. She knew Judson would be worrying for her, but she needed some clarity.

Even though she had nothing to do with the dark events happening to the witches of late, she felt responsible. What if the townspeople didn't believe her or the ones who had previously stood up for her and her family? If something didn't resolve soon, would they force the Blackstones to leave their new home and the town they helped build? And if they left, what about her brother and rogue witch hunter, Dante, who would stop at nothing to find them and try to "rehabilitate" them toward his way of life or extinguish them from theirs? It would all be for nothing—leaving Virginia, the cross-country travels by wagon train, those they had lost along the way, and all they had gone through for the new way of life they had acquired.

Furious at her current situation, Marie stood, wrapped her shawl tight around her shoulders, and paced in front of the fire.

"No, this can't be. I won't let it be the end. I trust my abilities and what I sense. I will do all I can to resolve the situation and find out what is going on in this town," Marie chanted, over and over like a mantra, until she believed it and felt strong and sure of herself once more. She needed to rise out of her downward mental spiral. She stopped in her tracks and gave herself a sharp nod. Newly determined, she left the den and promised herself she would pursue the source in the morning.

# CHAPTER 10

*T*he next day Marie woke with a renewed sense of purpose fueled by her resolve from the night before. She kept some of her plan to herself because she knew Judson wouldn't let her go out on her own, especially after Anne-Marie had told them not to at their Court meeting. She did feel bad about not abiding by Anne-Marie's request to stay with others, but she knew in her gut she had to seek out the threat, and she couldn't endanger anyone else.

Marie spotted Ric and Gaby Kasun near the Haven Saloon and altered her direction straight for them. She had an idea and wanted to ask them their opinion. Of course, by speaking to Gaby—who sat in on the meetings with the Court as a representative of the shifters even though the Kasuns hadn't traveled with them in the caravan—she would be divulging her plan and putting herself at risk to be stopped. Or perhaps she could get Gaby on her side.

"Good afternoon, Ric and Gaby," she said with a smile, like it was any other day.

"Hello, Marie. Nice to see you today," Gaby replied for them both.

"I'm glad I ran into you. I was actually hoping to ask you a few questions, if you have a moment?" Marie asked.

"Of course, Marie, go ahead." Ric inclined his head, suggesting she proceed.

"Thank you. First, I am wondering if you can tell me any information from your tracking the other night," she said quietly, in case anyone nearby could hear.

Ric and Gaby's gazes quickly shot to each other then back to her. "Marie, why do you ask?" Ric asked.

"We ran into you that night, and I admit I'm curious if you found anything."

"No, we didn't find much, to be honest. But the Luna Coven has asked us to keep things we find to ourselves—outside of informing them first—so as not to stir up any fear in the town," Ric explained.

"Even from those of us on the Court?" Marie was now skeptical.

"I don't agree, but for now, we tell them first," Gaby offered.

"No, that doesn't sound right to me at all." Marie frowned.

"To be fair, I think it is to keep the focus off you and your family. There were members of the Court who were quite suspicious of you. And while we believe you and your family are innocent, we are trying to keep the collateral damage to a minimum."

"I hear that, Ric. And while I appreciate the thought to protect us, I mean to solve this mystery and remove the suspicion on my family all together," Marie said, a little more adamantly than she intended. After all, the Kasuns were simply doing as they were asked, as protectors of the town.

"I caution you to not get too close. If you are in the wrong location at the wrong time, you will be implicated, and the town would be further on edge. People do crazy things when they are afraid and unsure. They fear what they do not understand and will jump to conclusions based on anything just to have someone to blame, even if they are innocent," Gaby warned.

"I promise to be careful, Gaby. Thank you for your concern, but I can't let this go. It is in my soul, in my very being, to pursue this to the end." Marie pressed her hand to her chest as she spoke. "With all the dreams I've been having, I feel I'm involved one way or another, so I'd rather be a part of the solution than sit by and let more bad things continue to happen to the witches of this town and anyone else it might involve."

Marie didn't know how else to end their conversation, as they wouldn't be agreeing, so she turned on her heels and began to walk away.

"Marie," Gaby said with a hushed tone as she came up alongside her. "I will do what I can to back you up in any way if I am able and free to do so. I would do the same in your situation. Your actions are admirable and should be assisted, not shut out to keep you safe."

Marie reacted without thinking, flinging her arms around Gaby's neck and giving her a hug. "Thank you," she whispered, then left without further words.

Marie continued her quest for information around the town to see if anyone had heard of anything strange or out of the ordinary. She assumed she probably stirred up some kind of trouble with the Court by asking questions, but she needed the info. She couldn't explain why, but in her soul she felt time was running out. The feeling was an annoyance that wouldn't leave her alone. It pressed upon her heart that if she didn't find out something soon, another witch would be endangered, and they could be more than simply drained this time. That thought caused Marie to wonder why the girl they came across the day before near the alley was left alive and not taken. She was grateful, but wondered about the cause. Had whoever captured the girl been interrupted? Did they not actually need the energy? How did they consume it? What were they doing with it?

Marie found herself in front of the temporary setup on the west side of the town square. The small wood shop was used by the Lancasters. The Lancasters were a family of witches, newer to town, invited by the Augustines. The Lancasters made potions, candles, and various soaps and scents and sold them from the wood shop that resembled more of a shack. Mr. Lancaster— Rufus, Marie thought his name was—worked on their more permanent shop residence nearby in his spare time. Even if she didn't already know he was a witch, the magical essence she sensed from him in the form of tingles shooting up her arms would have told her the truth.

"Mr. Lancaster?" she called to him as she approached cautiously in case he was unnerved by her presence. Marie hated that she suddenly felt on the defense, like she was indeed guilty of something. She stood taller and inhaled sharply through her nose. She would not be intimidated by even the imaginary feelings that plagued her mind because of the uncertainty she entertained.

He smiled at her approach, which relaxed her into a returning smile.

"Hello, Marie. What can I do for you today? Are you looking for a particular scent or tincture? We have a new batch the missus just whipped up." He gave her a toothy grin and with the gesture of a hand, invited her into his lean-to shop reinforced with magic to keep it standing.

"Thank you, Mr. Lancaster. I've only come to ask you a question or two, if you're not in the middle of anything," Marie clarified.

"Shoot, little lady," Rufus encouraged. He was a kind older gentleman who had been around town only a short time. It was becoming harder to keep track of all the new people coming into the town. She thought she might mention to Anne-Marie that they come up with a way to do so. Perhaps they could use amulets or something with a magical brand of sorts.

Marie smiled and nodded. "Mr. Lancaster, I'm sure you've heard reference to the young girl we found yesterday and the other missing wi—um, people recently." She paused and gauged his reaction to ensure he had indeed heard the news. Since his family were witches, he should have been notified to be on the lookout. He slowly nodded. "I'm helping find who is behind it all, and I'm wondering if you have any information that could be relevant. Has anything strange gone on with you or your family? Have you heard or even sensed anything out of the ordinary?"

"Now, Ms. Beaumont has already come by and asked questions of a similar nature, and I didn't have anything to tell her then. But earlier this morning, we had a disturbance of the wards on our barn. The ones around our home are solid as a rock, but mind you, we didn't think to make the ones around the property as strong. So the wards alerted us of an intruder, but we didn't find anyone. It was like a ghost came to pay us a visit. Now, Mrs. Lancaster doesn't think that's the case, but I didn't find anyone or anything disturbed. I think they might have just been testing the wards to see how close they could get." He frowned, then looked to Marie. "Do you think they were after our girls?"

Marie's expression soured. "I think it's possible, but we don't know what exactly this person—or people—want, let alone why they are targeting those they have. I'm sorry, Mr. Lancaster, but I suggest you strengthen your wards as soon as you can."

"Already done, Miss Marie. No one is getting onto my property without a major problem hitting them in the face." Mr. Lancaster chuckled to himself. Marie could only guess what kind of ward he set; it probably included some kind of hex to their physical person to point them out.

"I'm glad for you. Thank you for your time, Mr. Lancaster. Please let me or the Court know if you have any other situations or hear of anything that could be helpful."

He agreed and waved Marie on her way down the dirt and cobblestone street, but before she got too far, a group of young witches and mages, appearing unruly and angered, emerged from behind a structure.

# CHAPTER 11

Marie stopped and smiled as the group emerged from the area between two structures, where they had apparently been waiting for her. Her heart rate accelerated, but she refused to let them see her fear. Some of them were teenagers she knew, and she knew the parents of others. For some reason, they thought to take it upon themselves to confront her. What would they do to her? Possibly scare her, sure. But there in broad daylight, in front of several townspeople nearby—all she had to do was shout or scream and someone would surely come to help. But Marie would not be threatened.

"Hello! It's a fine day to be enjoying the outdoors, wouldn't you say, Jon? I had a nice chat with your parents just the other night."

Marie caught them off guard. Some of them faltered in their steps toward her and pretended to casually be hanging around. But others decided they'd rather have a confrontation.

"You need to stay away from us and the others in our group," a young man spat. Marie noted his choice of words, thankfully keeping the public in the dark about the witches and their coven.

"You need to show some respect, Denny. You don't know

what you're talking about," Rachael said, charging up with Ahote hot on her trail as they came to stand with Marie. Denny reared his head back as if he'd been slapped, seeing that another witch would stand against him and side with a lowly witch hunter. Denny was a member of the Green Coven, and Marie didn't know him other than by face, but she had a feeling Martha Daryn's attitude ran rampant in that group.

Marie placed her hand on Rachael's arm, letting her know she didn't think the confrontation was worth the spectacle they were about to create. Marie turned her head to smile at Ahote and noticed a few others had joined to stand behind her, including Mr. Lancaster and his wife. Also among them was a young woman in her early twenties, whom Marie didn't recognize, but based on the low-level vibe she received, the woman was half witch. Marie appreciated her stance with her and smiled at her even though she didn't know who she was. Marie glanced at her face quickly to reassure herself that the girl was indeed already half witch—not that she'd been drained like the other girl who hadn't been quite so lucky to still be half witch. Marie chose to trust her hunter gifts, but still she hoped for a chance to speak with the girl once the group confrontation subsided.

Thankfully, at that moment, Sheriff Ric Kasun and a few other members of the Kasun pack stepped out of the saloon and moved in her direction to be a strong presence in case the situation got out of hand. The group's eyes widened upon seeing them, and several stepped away almost instantly.

"I guess they don't want to stand up to the sheriff . . . or maybe it was the idea of a snarling pack of wolves on their tails," Marie whispered to Rachael, who stood so close she would hear her.

"I think they'd rather not have their parents get wind of their involvement," she said with a chuckle.

"That too." Marie snickered.

"I hope there was no trouble here," Ric Kasun said as he walked up to Marie.

"No, at least not yet. I think they were trying to scare me, though," she admitted.

"I'm sorry, Marie. You and your family don't deserve that. We need to catch the culprit soon or I'm afraid the town is going to lose all sense of its values and camaraderie.

"I agree."

Sheriff Kasun signaled for his guys to head out, leaving Marie and those with her standing in the road. She turned to thank those who came to support her. She felt drawn to the girl she saw and wanted a chance to talk to her. But when she looked for her, she was gone.

"Thank you for being here with us, Mr. And Mrs. Lancaster." She turned to Rachael and Ahote. "Thanks, your timing was perfect." Marie took a deep breath.

"Of course, dear. We know you have nothing to do with any of those disappearances," Mrs. Lancaster said with a sweet smile.

"Thank you. Did by chance any of you see the young woman with you—slender build, pale with red hair?" Marie asked. "I'm not sure who she was, but she's gone now. I was hoping to talk with her."

Rachael and Ahote both shook their heads.

"Are you seeing ghosts now?" Rachael teased, and looped her arm with Marie's.

She laughed. "I don't think so. No, wait, I felt her. She was either drained or she had to have been half witch."

"Let me know if you see her again, and I can find out who she is. Maybe she's a part of the Green Coven or new to town," Rachael mentioned.

The Lancasters returned to their shop and took the vibrant essence of their magical energy with them, relieving Marie of most of the tingles shooting up and down her arms. She had been around Rachael so long, the usual sensations she felt from having her around were normal by this point. More often than not, it was unusual to not have any feelings at all when she was away from Rachael.

"Oh, Marie! There's Mrs. Brouchard just over there. She's one of the friendlier witches in the Green Coven. Maybe she knows your mystery girl," Rachael excitedly said.

"Lead the way. You might be more welcome to ask questions than I would at this stage," Marie admitted sadly.

"Cheer up. We'll get this figured out in no time. And then they'll all be sorry and owe you lots of gifts," Rachael said with a wink.

Marie laughed, which she knew was Rachael's intent. "I'd like that," Marie teasingly returned. "They should bring gifts."

"Why would they bring gifts?" Ahote asked, confused, making the girls laugh even more.

# CHAPTER 12

W alking past the saloon, Marie let Rachael approach Mrs. Brouchard while she and Ahote stood slightly back to give them space. But then a lovely surprise happened.

"Marie, Ahote, come join us. You don't need to be shy," Mrs. Brouchard said, waving them forward. Marie's shoulders relaxed. She hadn't realized how tense she was, ready for someone else to doubt her and judge her without proof. It was one thing for someone to come against her for something she believed in. She was used to that from her siblings who chose to go rogue with her brother Dante. But for someone to affront her just for being who and what she was, was a hit on the lowest level. She vowed never to do that to anyone going forward.

Marie smiled and casually waved as she approached. "It's so good to see you, Mrs. Brouchard."

"It's good to see you as well." The woman smiled. She was older than Marie and Rachael, probably in her fifties, but with the witches, one could never truly tell. "Rachael was just telling me you had a question regarding one of the members of our coven. Is that right?"

"Yes. Earlier a girl—maybe in her early twenties—joined our group to stand up to some annoyances, and I wanted to thank her, but she took off before I could say anything. I'm wondering if you might know who she is. She was slender with shoulder-length red hair and fair skin. I believe she is half witch. Might you know whom I am referring to?" Marie asked.

The woman considered for a moment before her eyes widened. "Oh dear, how could I forget? Yes, you must be speaking of Cynthia Walvern. She was always an interesting girl in her youth. I'd imagine she is about twenty-one or twenty-two now."

"That seems about right," Marie agreed. "Do you know anything else about her?"

"All I know is that she was very smart and wanted to learn skills in the medical field. She was only half witch, and her powers didn't do much for her, if I remember right. Her mom had mentioned something of the sort, in confidence of course."

"Of course," Rachael encouraged, though Marie knew her response was sarcastic.

"So she left not long after they had arrived. They had only been in town a short time. I think she was having trouble with some of the other younger witches, since she wasn't a very competent witch herself and couldn't compete with them."

"Wait just a minute," Rachael interrupted. "Just because she is half witch doesn't mean she is a lesser person. Maybe she needed proper tutelage or a differing perspective. And perhaps your other more *competent* youths were bullying and crushing her spirit. I don't blame her for leaving if that's why."

The woman looked affronted, as Marie knew she would. "Well, I—that seems to be a bit of an overreaction!" Mrs. Brouchard hissed. "Just because you *could have* been a coven leader had your mother not died does not mean you *should have*!" Rachael reared back as if slapped in the face. "Oh, yes, I know about you and your unruly magic. What's left of your coven is better off working with the more established ones in this town."

"How dare you! My mother was killed. Not that it's your business, but I have mastered my magic! And at least I'm not a pompous arse of a woman!" Rachael yelled back.

The woman had no words. She turned and marched away with a swish of her bustled dress and threw her sash around her shoulders with her head held too high as she went to meet friends down the road.

"That went well. You really are coming along with your people skills, Rach," Marie said with unbridled sarcasm.

Fuming, Rachael growled under her breath and placed her hands on her hips.

"Breathe, my little fighter," Ahote soothed, stroking her arm, and she began to calm.

"Excuse me," a small feminine voice called from behind the side wall of the saloon. They all turned to see the very girl they sought peering around the corner. Her green eyes were wide with surprise, set against a creamy yet speckled complexion; her eyes reflected having seen too much in her short lifespan, but she still held a glimmer of hope. Her wavy red locks were cut abruptly at her shoulders, and she appeared much too thin. "I couldn't help but overhear what you said on my behalf. Thank you. No one has ever stood up for me before."

Rachael quickly moved forward, and Marie was right behind her. "She was out of line," Rachael said, then continued, "I'm Rachael Stronghold, and this is Marie Blackstone. Who are you?"

The girl gave them each a small smile. "Cynthia."

"Thank you for standing with me earlier, Cynthia. You don't even know me, but I appreciated it," Marie added.

"No one should be pushed around, but especially by that lot. They are babied brats and deserve whatever they get," she said with unexpected vehemence. At seeing their surprise, Cynthia shrugged her shoulders and admitted, "They bullied me when I used to live here. I don't have any kind feelings for them."

"I understand that," Rachael offered, to put the girl at ease.

They chatted for a little bit and introduced her to Ahote before they decided to continue their walk through the rest of town.

"I heard you asking some questions, trying to find out who is behind those witches being taken," Cynthia admitted. "I would like to help you find the bad guy. No one should be picked on, and I want to have a chance to be the heroine in this story."

Marie paused. She felt a little strange to hear the girl had been essentially following them to know she'd been asking questions. But if she had gone through what Cynthia had, perhaps she'd want to be careful about who she talked to and want to find out information about them beforehand too.

Marie glanced around them to ensure no one was close enough to listen. "I feel I should tell you: I've been warned to not pursue this. I can't stop you, but you need to know what you're getting into and the possible dangers."

"I'm well aware there could be danger, but I think I can cover myself enough, even only being a half witch. I want to help."

"I also feel I should tell you I am a non-practicing witch hunter. I can guarantee your safety from me, but that's about it," Marie said honestly, then quickly looked away as if suddenly the girl's reaction mattered to her.

"I know who you are, Marie," was all she said in reply, as if it didn't matter to her. Marie smiled as an invisible weight left her shoulders.

"Okay then, let's see if we can find any clues to solve our mystery," Rachael declared, patting Marie on the back.

"I think we have investigated almost every area around the main part of the town here. Perhaps it's time to expand the search a little farther out." Marie pointed in the direction of the closest wooded area.

"The forest?" Cynthia asked. Her footing became unstable and she almost tripped, but Marie caught her elbow to help steady her. "Thank you," she breathed with a sigh of relief.

Marie received the familiar yet weakened sensation from a witch she normally did, but something caught her off guard—a feeling of nothingness, a void within the girl's being. Marie caught herself before she gave some kind of telling reaction. She didn't want to make Cynthia feel uneasy, but she wanted to know what the other half of her being was. Marie had assumed half witch, half human. But currently, she had to guess she was something other than human. But what?

"It's not far, and we won't even go inside the forest, since it's starting to get dark. But we can walk the perimeter and see if there are any clues."

"What kind of clues are we looking for?" she asked Rachael.

"Anything, really," Marie supplied instead. "Anything that strikes you as odd or out of place. I know Sheriff Kasun and his patrol are searching the woods, and they'd know for sure if anything was out there, but I just have a feeling I'm supposed to."

"Let's do it, then," Cynthia said enthusiastically, complete with arm gestures.

"What do you think, Ahote? You've been quiet," Rachael said, reaching for her husband's hand.

"I think it is a good idea. I think there is danger afoot. Keep our eyes open," he said.

The four of them remained silent as they walked the edge along the treed area south of town, listening and watching their surroundings. Marie cast out her senses often but came back with nothing in the realm of any other witches in the vicinity or any kind of black or dark magic, at least in the area they covered.

"There's nothing here," she finally admitted.

"Let's go back and come up with a new plan," Rachael offered, trying to keep Marie's hopes up.

"No, that's enough for today I think—" Marie whipped her head in the opposite direction. "Wait . . ." She stopped and narrowed her eyes, looking deep into the woods. She closed her eyes and let her senses stretch out. "I feel something, something dark, but it's faint." Marie gripped her stomach with one hand and rubbed her forearm with the other. Suddenly, she cursed a word she hardly used and stood straight. "It's gone already. What is going on with my senses?"

"It's okay, Marie. You'll find it again," Cynthia said with reassuring confidence, reaching out to touch Marie's arm, but it hung in the air momentarily as she changed her mind and let her hand drop.

"Thanks, Cyn, I hope so—can I call you Cyn?" she asked, unsure.

"Actually, I prefer Cynthia." Cynthia slowly backed away. "I need to go. I'm sorry. I just remembered I told my mom I would be back by now. She worries. Thank you for letting me hunt with you for a bit. Can I join you another time?" She kept backing away.

"Of course," Marie said, watching her leave with confusion. Just before Cynthia turned, Marie caught a flash in her eyes. Marie blinked. She could've sworn she saw her eyes change color, or grow darker at least. Weird. Now she really wanted to know what her other half could be.

"That was oddly abrupt," Rachael said, and Marie nodded.

Not even a few minutes later, they were stopped by a woman in a housedress tying her bonnet around her head and under her chin as she ran out to meet them.

"Marie Blackstone?" she asked.

Marie nodded. "Yes, I am she. What is going on?"

The woman panted, slightly out of breath, but quickly recovered. She also was a witch. "Anne-Marie asked me to collect you. The young girl"—she quickly assessed who was with Marie and if she should be transparent or not—"who passed out the other day has awakened. She thought you might want to meet her and sit in on the questioning."

Marie's face lit up. "It's such good news she woke up! And yes, please, I would very much like to be present for that." Turning to Rachael and Ahote, she asked, "Would you mind terribly if I caught up with you later or at home?"

"Of course not. We will see you at home unless it's past dark; then I'll send Judson for you."

# CHAPTER 13

*M*arie hadn't received one clue or found a piece of evidence since they had gone into the main part of town a couple days ago. The inaction and the unknown was driving her crazy. The meeting with the girl who returned to consciousness was a failure—other than her waking up. Marie was so grateful for her state of being, but unfortunately, the girl couldn't remember anything but black eyes and the feeling of being sucked into a small hole. She was still so weak and frail. That information really wasn't much to go on, but did confirm the energy parasite they had previously discussed.

Something was building. Something was coming. She could feel it. Her dreams had gone silent. The witches hadn't reported anyone else being abducted. Whoever had been taking them was biding their time—or they had left town, but Marie didn't think so. But why? If, as she suspected, the creature needed a witch's essence to sustain itself or survive, then it was only a matter of time. But if the being needed the magic for a specific purpose, then perhaps the project had been completed and it no longer needed their energy. She attempted to make a list of the creatures that could need that magic, but unfortunately it was a small list—what does one even call an energy vampire?

Marie made her way into the kitchen to make her and Judson lunch. Their kitchen was beyond anything they had in the past. The black cast iron wood stove made her smile as well as heated the room. Having a witch in the house was an added bonus, as she could help remove the soot from the draperies and the walls with a simple spell.

Rachael was bent over at the fireplace, stirring soup in the large black cauldron positioned above the flames. "Rachael, have you seen Judson?"

Rachael straightened up and glanced over at Marie. She paused for a moment. "I think he said he was going to be at the forge working on something."

"My dagger, probably. Some of the metal detail work was wearing thin. He's fixing it—again," Marie explained with a smile, but then her hand flew to her chest, and she sharply inhaled. "Judson," she whispered, and ran out the front door.

Something was wrong, but she wasn't sure what. What she felt wasn't because of her witch hunter abilities, but more a gut reaction from her connection to Judson. She ran across the expanse of the back of their property, and out of the corner of her eye, she spotted Cynthia awkwardly pacing outside their land. Marie did a double take to ensure she truly saw her.

"Cynthia! I don't have time to stop. Come with me!" Marie shouted and waved Cynthia to follow her. Marie was first to burst through the doors of the temporary blacksmith shop. Her eyes scanned the room and quickly found Judson at work on her dagger by the fire pit, sticking it into the bucket of water to cool the work he had just accomplished.

"Judson? Is everything okay?" Marie asked, her chest heaving as she sucked air into her lungs once more while her heart beat out of control.

Judson's expression suggested he had no idea what she spoke of. "I believe so. Are you okay, Marie?"

He set the dagger down and rushed to her, placing both

hands around her upper arms, seeking out what could possibly be wrong with her.

"I had a feeling. Something wasn't right, and I had to come check."

Judson cocked his head. "Unless you had a premonition and something was about to go wrong with the fire and you stopped me before it happened, nothing was out of the usual out here."

Marie frowned. "So weird. My instincts have been all over the place. Maybe you're right. Perhaps we prevented something."

Judson glanced over her shoulder as the door clicked shut. "Hello," he said awkwardly with a confused smile. "Can we help you?"

"Oh, Judson, this is Cynthia. The girl I mentioned we ran into the other day in town. I found her outside on my way here." Marie turned to Cynthia and waved her forward. "Cynthia, this is my husband Judson. He does the best iron work in town, if you ever need anything made."

Cynthia smiled. "I'll remember that. It's nice to meet you, sir."

"Likewise," Judson responded. "I'd shake your hand, but I'm a bit of a mess." Judson raised up his hands, palms out, to display his grime from the morning's work.

"I'll take Cynthia with me to fetch some lunch for you. Carry on with your work." Marie shooed him away.

"Can I watch for a moment? I've never seen metalwork in progress." Cynthia's eyes were wide with curiosity.

"It is quite fascinating," Marie admitted with a wide smile. "Sure. We'll stay quiet, Judson, just for a bit, then we'll let you work."

Judson went back to the fire pit and picked up the dagger.

"Soot yourself." He chuckled to himself.

"Wow, he gets a new audience and is already trying to be funny." Marie waved him off and rolled her eyes for Cynthia's benefit, to which the young woman giggled.

"I like you two. Most married couples your age end up being too serious too soon and then they just grow old."

"I think the struggle is that life gets serious out here in the wild, and people have to grow up fast. We've been blessed to truly enjoy each other's company and our life together, even when it's been hard."

Judson heated the next piece he needed to work on: a long sword that had a chip in the blade. He stuck the sword into the fire to heat and soften the metal. When he pulled it out, he lifted his hammer and began to work. The sounds of metal striking metal echoed through the shed. Sparks of red and orange flew through the air at the contact.

Marie glanced over at Cynthia. Her wide eyes reflected the dancing of the flames, which quickly turned to something more awkward. Marie watched Judson again, trying to see him through the eyes of someone younger who didn't know him. He wore an old work shirt he had ripped the sleeves off of for better arm movement, which also exposed his defined and muscular arms. He also wore a full leather apron that hugged his body. His tanned skin was slick and dirty with the heat and grime of the room. She and Judson had known each other since they were young, but suddenly Marie fell for him all over again. When she observed Cynthia watching her husband once more, she felt pride that her man was quite the specimen to look at, but at the same time a pang of jealousy. She didn't know Cynthia yet, but she didn't think the girl would disrespect her right in front of her. Either way, it was time to leave.

Marie cleared her throat, and Cynthia had the grace to blush. "It's okay. He is quite fascinating. Look but don't touch," Marie offered a friendly warning and wink. Cynthia giggled but nodded her understanding.

A clatter sounded behind them, and both turned quickly to see what had happened. Judson had knocked off a couple tools next to him on the ridge of the fire pit. Looking at Judson's face, he seemed confused by what had happened.

Cynthia made a strangled sound from her throat, like she was choking.

"Cynthia, are you all right?" Marie asked, so confused about what was going on.

"I have to go. I'm sorry." Cynthia's eyes flashed from vibrant green to a dark dulled color, almost black, then she swiftly ran out the door without another word.

Marie didn't have time to think more on it as she turned back to Judson, shock on her face when she saw him.

"Judson," she whispered with awe. Not only were there sparks from the fire as he continued to strike the metal, but blue and green sparks came from his hands, blending into the montage of the sparks flying. Marie felt it then again.

Magic. But also a debilitating sense of black magic.

"Judson? What's happening?" she said louder, barely able to get the words out, clutching her stomach.

Judson came out of whatever trance he had been in while diving into the rhythm of his work. His eyes grew wide with shock. He apparently had no idea he was doing it. Unintentional magic emanated from him.

*But how?* He wasn't a witch—at least not that they had known.

"Marie? What am I doing? How is this happening?" he asked, panic lacing his words. "I thought it was from the aether in the water from the falls."

"Judson, I *felt* you." Her words held as much shock as her face.

He looked at her inquisitively.

"I mean, I felt you as I feel *witches*."

Neither of them spoke for a few moments. The weight of the situation grew heavier and heavier the longer they stared into each other's eyes. No one moved.

"I'm not a witch," Judson finally said.

"I think that may not be true. Perhaps we need to talk to the

Luna Coven. I think they have ways of testing this sort of thing, don't they? Didn't your mom's coven?"

Judson slowly nodded, his face pale and his gaze distant. He appeared to be in shock. He still held his hammer with a white-knuckled grip until he realized it and let it slip to the ground.

Marie vaguely wondered if Cynthia had seen Judson's sparks and it caught her off guard. Being a witch herself, it shouldn't have scared her, but maybe she, too, felt the dark magic Marie had. But that was something she couldn't comprehend at the moment.

# CHAPTER 14

arie, Judson, and Rachael rode into town on their horse and buggy to arrive faster. Rachael had spelled a bird to deliver a message to Anne-Marie to inform her of their arrival and ask to have the high council of the Luna Coven with her. Ahote would stay with their little one while Hank, Rodney, Michael, and Caroline worked the vines, preparing them for winter in the Blackstones' vineyard for the new winery they were about to open. The first run of wines in a variety of reds and whites was in the process of being tested. Life had to carry on, and Judson ensured them they wouldn't be gone long.

Pulling up to the mansion where the Court held their meetings, Judson got out and shakily tied the horse to the post. The three of them walked up the front steps. Priscilla Augustine opened the front door and welcomed them with an understanding smile and showed them inside. No one seemed to know what to say while they awaited Anne-Marie.

Not even a minute after they sat, Anne-Marie entered the house.

"Marie, Judson, what seems to be happening? Rachael was vague with her missive, which I understand. The birds tend to confuse information if too many details are given." She winked at Rachael, attempting to alleviate some of the tension in the room.

Marie took a deep breath and began on her husband's behalf. "For some time now, I've noticed Judson struggling with something personal, but when we finally addressed it, he believed it had something to do with working with the aether from the falls and my family's stone in the dagger. It made sense to me at the time, but then I started *feeling* him as I do with you all." She glanced around the room at all the witches present—the Augustines, both Raffaele and Priscilla; Rodavan Bishop; Rachael, of course; and a few others. She also noted Elsmed Fairchild's presence because, of course, the mansion was his home.

"Judson, can you share your experience with this?" Raffaele asked.

Judson nodded. He wrung his hands, then wiped them on his pants before standing up, clearly uncomfortable. "As you know, I grew up in the Stronghold coven back east in Virginia. My mother was a witch, but I was adopted into her family. Or so I was told. I have never had any magic to speak of. When we arrived here and I started using the water from the falls, I began to have some strange things happen. Sparks would fly when I was intently working on something. I assumed it was the water having some kind of strange effect on me as I worked. I began to feel other sensations that were new, but they were very subtle and didn't go very far. I couldn't make anything happen. I remembered some spells from my youth and even went as far as to try some, but nothing happened. In fact, I gained pains in my head instead. Today, I worked in the forge almost as if in a trance, then I awoke to blue and green sparks coming from my hands, and I hadn't been working with the aether." He looked at his hands, then to each of them for an answer. "Can any of you explain what's happening?"

Anne-Marie offered him a small knowing smile. "Judson, we

have a test we can perform to check your heritage—whether you have witch blood or not. I'm certain, however, your coven back home would have had this same test. I also asked Elsmed to be here. He has a gift to ensure the honesty and validity of our thoughts and memories. If you let him, he can perform his own sort of test to see if we can determine what happened in your past based on suppressed memories you may have."

"Yes, to both!" Judson said enthusiastically. "Any information we can gain would be helpful, thank you."

Marie grabbed his hand and squeezed him tight in support.

Anne-Marie nodded and gestured for the witches to stand. In her hands she held a small bowl. "Judson, please stand in the middle. If you could give me a strand of your hair from your head and a drop of your blood, I will mix it with a special revealing powder I created. As we surround you, I will say a spell."

Without hesitation, Judson yanked a hair from his head and gave it to her. Then he pulled out a small knife from his pocket, but Rodavan stopped him with his hand outstretched and an exasperated look.

"Please use this." He handed him an athame—a knife used in rituals, most likely cleansed and purified to use in such a situation. Judson accepted it with an appreciative look. He didn't even flinch when he poked the tip of his thumb.

Anne-Marie held out her mortar for him to allow several drops to fall in. She then added her powder, blended it all together with the pestle, and the witches began to chant. Judson held still in the center of the circle.

Marie watched with a hint of nervousness for her husband. One way or another, they would find something, and she hoped it wasn't more than her loving Judson could handle.

A moment later, the chant ceased. Anne-Marie stepped in front of Judson and smeared the paste she created of powder and Judson's hair and blood onto his forehead. The blood sizzled and popped the moment it touched his skin, and he flinched.

"Be calm, Judson," she reprimanded. "Elsmed, please step forward and conduct your test."

Elsmed, with his stoic, unreadable expression, took his place in front of Judson. Marie always felt uncomfortable around Elsmed, although he had never given her reason to feel that way. She had always felt he was looking into her soul and could read her life story without her permission—she supposed he actually could, but she didn't like not knowing what he saw. She'd rather he simply asked her to share it. But now she wondered more than ever if Judson had a history hidden from him.

"Open your eyes, Judson. I need to read your soul," Elsmed instructed with a flat tone. Judson did as he said and allowed Elsmed to truly look into his history. Marie admired her husband's bravery.

Only a moment later did Elsmed blink and take a step back, indicating he was finished. Everyone looked to him for his response, but he looked to Anne-Marie first.

She nodded. "Judson, based on my test of magic, yes, you have witch blood. And always have." She looked at Elsmed.

He also nodded but added, "Based on my findings, I agree you have always had witch blood. The woman you knew as your mother was actually your aunt, caring for you when your mother died in childbirth. They didn't want you to carry the weight of feeling it was your fault she died. Your father was also a witch—a powerful one, based on what I saw. I do not know who he is, but he was not present. Feuding covens, I believe."

"Why didn't he have power until now?" Marie interrupted.

Elsmed gave her a look suggesting he was about to get there. "There is a spell on him to lock down his magic lest he ask questions they had no answers for. They thought they were doing what would be best for him. If the father knew he existed and had the power he does, the other coven would come for him and claim him for their own. Your aunt couldn't have handled that loss as well. She did her best to teach you all you would need to know without teaching it to you as a witch. Everything you need and are is within you. Anne-Marie and the coven simply need to unlock your magic."

"Thank you, sir," Judson said with an inclined head.

Elsmed took a step back, as if his job was done, and then he left the room.

"I believe your contact with the aether in the water was simply a catalyst to ignite your suppressed ancestry," Anne-Marie added.

Judson's face was a kaleidoscope of emotions. Marie came alongside him and held his hand in both of hers. She wanted him to feel all the love she had always had for him, plus even more.

"Are you ready to unlock your magic, Judson Carter Blackstone?" Raffaele stepped forward as he asked the question. Priscilla joined him and held his hand. Rachael, then Rodavan, did the same, and the others as well as Anne-Marie completed the circle around them both. Marie slowly inhaled, willing her body to remain in check with all the witches so close. Tingles shot up and down her arms, but she had control. After all, this moment was for Judson, and she wouldn't miss it for all the discomfort in the world.

"Yes, please unlock my past into my present as I become my future," Judson profoundly said into the silence of the room.

The room chanted as one, over and over. Their voices grew in strength and power until something in the atmosphere snapped and a bright light exploded before their eyes. Simple as that, Judson Blackstone became the first witch married to a witch hunter.

# CHAPTER 15

*J*ust before they left, Raffaele encouraged them to take some time for themselves and go for a walk to enjoy and absorb the magic of nature, especially for the new witch. It would give Judson some time to let the news and magic settle. So they did. Rachael accompanied them because they thought of her as family, and Judson had many witchy questions for her.

"Do you always feel this much energy constantly flowing through your system?" he asked first, as they entered into a wooded area past the mansion.

"No, I don't think so. Having always had my magic, I'm not sure what you're going through, Judson. I'm sorry. I believe what is happening is akin to an awakening, where everything is alive and surging with an incredible force but will settle as it merges with your body, mind, and spirit."

"What does it feel like, Jud?" Marie asked, curious as to all the new things her husband was experiencing.

He thought about it for a moment. "It feels like the adrenaline rush I get when I'm in a forging state, creating something beautiful from a piece of metal piping, but much more."

Marie squinted in his direction, attempting to understand that feeling.

"Maybe more like when you can sense a witch's magic, Marie, and it's very powerful, but instead of in your arms, it is all over your entire body," Rachael tried to help out.

"Good one, Rachael. Thanks. Yes, Marie, I think it might be like what you've described to me," Judson offered.

"That makes sense." She reached for his hand, and a twinkle lit her eyes. "Do you want to try some?"

Judson stopped. "Some what?"

"Magic, silly." Marie laughed. "Rachael's here. She could help guide you."

Judson's eyes lit up like a little boy at Christmas. Marie knew it had always been hard on him being the only one in the coven who couldn't do magic and always wanting to. Her heart melted at his unbridled excitement at finally being able to make a dream come true.

He turned to Rachael. "Would you help me?"

"Of course," Rachael said. Her smile reached from ear to ear. They stopped walking, and Rachael looked for and found a pine cone on the ground. She held it out in front of him. "Now, pretend this is a candle. Visualize it as a candle. Visualize your magic welling up within you, then traveling out from you to light the tip of this candle. Watch me first, then you try."

Judson nodded and stared at Rachael intently. Marie watched closely, silently cheering Judson on and wishing there was something she could do to help him. Rachael lit the pine cone candle with practiced ease, then extinguished the flame and turned to Judson. He took the candle and handed it to Marie, who smiled, grateful to have something to assist with.

"Focus, Jud. I know you can do this," Marie encouraged.

Judson's eyes narrowed, and his face scrunched up tight, but nothing happened. He blew out a frustrated breath and looked to the sky. "It's not working."

"No, of course not. You looked like you were constipated." Rachael and Marie both laughed. Judson also laughed and relaxed. "Now this time, relax. Magic is a part of who you are. Even if you are just realizing it. It's always been there. You are learning to connect with it. Try this: Visualize a box in the center of your being. In that box is all the power that is yours by birthright. Now mentally take your hand and open the box; reach inside and grasp the power. You don't need to rip it out. Just hold it in your hand. Claim it and allow it to travel throughout your body until it is ready to be used."

"It sounds like you personify your magic," Judson stated.

"I guess I do. It helps me to be one with my magic and gives me grace when it's not performing as I need it to." Rachael shrugged. "Okay, now try again. Remember to relax."

He nodded sharply and inhaled a deep, slow breath, then held it and peacefully released it. He gently focused on the pine cone candle, and a moment later, it sparked and sputtered until the flame caught. Judson whooped with excitement, and Marie allowed tears of happiness to stream down her face. Rachael beamed with pride.

Instantly, Marie doubled over, holding her stomach.

"Black magic," she rushed out, before she was debilitated. Rachael and Judson came around Marie, and the three of them were on guard.

"Where? Can you tell?" Rachael asked.

Marie nodded and tried to point straight ahead, but her hand shook with tremors.

"Of course she can tell," a feminine voice called haughtily from behind some bushes. A moment later, Cynthia sashayed confidently through the foliage. "She's been able to tell every time I show up. Lucky for me, she's so insecure, she doubted herself and her powers. As soon as she sensed me, I disappeared to encourage that doubt." Cynthia laughed, but it didn't sound like the young woman they had spent time with.

"Cynthia?" Rachael was confused. Cynthia shot a look at

Rachael, but instead of bright green, her eyes were shiny black orbs.

"I'm not Cynthia, not really," the woman who looked like Cynthia explained. "You see, I'm half Cynthia, but I'm also Cynder, her other half."

"Her other half?" Judson asked. "What do you mean?"

Marie had a brief moment of realization at why her other half felt like a void. It was full of darkness.

Cynthia—or Cynder—moved closer, her red shoulder-length wavy hair swaying with the movement. Cynthia had been more timid and didn't walk with such attitude. The sight was strangely comical. As soon as she realized she had done it, her power ebbed, and the beacon of dark magic that had shot out from her toned down. Marie could stand up straight and breathe more normally now.

"Apparently, I'm relegated to explaining everything in this life," Cynder said with annoyance, under her breath.

"This life? Who are you?" Rachael asked, more skeptical.

"I told you. I am Cynder, an alchemist from another land, but I am also so much more. I made great discoveries and found a way to preserve my life and put magic to good use."

"The magic is your energy source," Marie stated as understanding began to dawn on her.

"Very good, hunter. You and I have more in common than you would like to let on." Cynder lifted a corner of her lips and sneered at Marie.

"My brother maybe, but not me." Marie rushed out the question she'd been seeking the answer to. "What about the others? The witches . . . the ones you stole magical energy from —where are they?"

"I had no further use for them. If any of them are still alive . . . well, you'll never find them, so they might as well be dead."

Hope soared in Marie's chest that the witches might still be alive, if only drained of their magical energy. She also knew that to a witch, many would feel they would have rather been dead than have to live without their magic. Still, she would find them and see them back with their parents one way or another.

"How did you become half a person?" Judson asked curiously, not fully understanding what was happening.

"Half? Half a person?" Cynder shouted, anger rising to the surface and making her seem to grow taller. "We are a full person—we are more than a full person, with twice the abilities and powers."

"Calm down, Cynth—Cynder, please," Rachael pleaded with her. "We're trying to understand. Please tell us your story." Marie recognized she was buying them time, hopefully for help to arrive.

Cynder seemed to visibly shrink back down to her original size. "Rachael, you can be sensible when you want to. I *would* like to tell my story. No one ever wants to hear it. It began when this young and foolish girl came looking for the famed alchemist to assist her in her medical studies. I had already killed the alchemist and possessed his body at this point; she got in too deep and didn't realize what she was playing at when she released me. It was all too easy to possess her after that."

"And who were you before you assumed the role of the alchemist?" Marie asked.

"Apophis, a demon of chaos. But I had found it troubling to sustain myself in this life cycle on this world, until I met the alchemist. She was already doing advanced work, but no one would believe her or give her the time of day, especially being a woman. But now I have all her knowledge. However, her body held no strength as a human and began to wear out over time. This body, though . . ." Cynder gestured her hands awkwardly down her sides. "Cynthia's body is stronger, having witch blood. Though, I admit, I grow tired of her weariness. Had I known she was only half witch, I might not have bothered with her, but my prospects where we lived were meager. Now, I seek a stronger vessel to abide in." Cynder—

Apophis—Cynthia—whoever it was looked directly and hungrily at Judson.

"Oh, no, you don't." Marie stepped in front of him. "You don't get to come here and just take what or whomever you want."

"I think I do."

Marie gasped. "Look!"

She almost missed it. But Cynder's body blurred momentarily. And the green eyes of Cynthia suddenly showed through.

"Help!" she cried. "I'm so sorry. I don't have much time. I can't hold her off. I didn't realize the deal I was making. The alchemist promised me she had a way to restore me to full witch status if I assisted her in a project. I didn't realize I was the project. I know where they are . . ." Cynthia gasped for breath as if going under water, and her head shook repetitively before her body blurred again and the black eyes of Cynder returned.

"Cynthia is still in there," Rachael whispered. "We have to find a way to save her."

"Agreed," Marie rushed out.

Cynder stalked forward, her eyes locked on Judson. "Cynthia will never get out. She made her bed."

"Why . . . why do you want him and not me?" Rachael stammered, changing the subject.

Cynder flashed her eyes in Rachael's direction. "Because, you foolish woman, he is a newborn witch. His power is at its strongest and most unruly. His magic calls to me." She physically licked her lips. Hunger sparked in her eyes—hunger for his raw magic.

"Just let her try," Judson said, taking a fighter's stance and holding up his fists in defense.

"Judson! Don't antagonize her," Marie whisper-shouted. "I can't help if the darkness takes over." Fear ran down Marie's spine as she thought of her dream.

"The darkness will ultimately take this whole town, then move on to the next one," Cynder said with an evil laugh.

"No, it won't. We will stop you." Marie faced off with the two-part being, but it only continued to laugh, seeming more evil as it did. As a demonstration of Cynder's growing power, she shot a stream of lightning out from her hand and into a nearby tree, splitting it in half lengthwise. Everyone ducked.

"What do we do?" Rachael whispered fast, while the noise of the tree splintering covered their voices.

"Distract her. I sense witches coming," Marie said. Marie didn't actually sense the witches coming yet. She hoped they would, but she didn't know what they were going to do or how to get out of it all safe and sound. So she improvised to give Judson and Rachael courage. They were a ragtag crew: a hunter with no physical powers, a witch whose magic didn't always cooperate, and a new witch with no idea yet what he was doing. But Marie couldn't let them know she feared for them. She suddenly had renewed faith in her own abilities, realizing that they never were on the outs, but were being manipulated by Cynder's darkness.

"How do you harness control of both your powers and Cynthia's witch powers at the same time?" Judson asked, trying to get her talking so she wouldn't blow anything else up.

"Cynthia is puny. I have no trouble controlling her measly powers. She was weak. That was how I was able to so easily convince her to help me. However, her witch ability with lightning is a handy trick." She stalked forward. "But you, Judson—I can sense the strength of your magic from here. It wafts to me and smells so delicious. You and me, we could do terrible things together." She licked her lips once more.

The action was so reprehensible, Marie wanted to throw up.

"She is not puny, and she is not weak!" Rachael stepped in front of Judson and waved her hands around. She threw out a spell, and a rope appeared and wrapped itself around Cynder. Rachael tried to restrain her, but Cynder used the power Cynthia had with the elements and set fire to the rope, which quickly burned.

"You dare to restrain me?" Cynder yelled.

"Cynthia, I know you're still in there," Rachael shouted at the top of her lungs. "If you can hear me, I need you to try to take control again. We need you to fight back. Take control of your power and your life. Fight with us. We can help you!" A single tear slowly traced the contour of Rachael's cheek on its way to the tip of her chin, then down to the ground. Marie knew Rachael wanted to save the young witch, but she didn't see how it was possible at this juncture. "We can free you from this monster!"

Suddenly Marie had an idea—something she had read in her family's journal, something she never thought she would need to know.

Cynder swiped her hand violently to the side, sending a gust of wind toward Rachael. The wind picked her up and threw her hard against the trunk of a tree. She fell to the ground with a loud thud. She lay there unmoving, barely breathing.

"NO!" screamed Marie. She ran to her best friend—her sister—and fell down beside her.

A moment later, the cavalry came through the woods behind them, in the form of the Luna Coven and some of the most powerful witches the town had, along with a few others of immense power.

# CHAPTER 16

Seeing Rachael lying on the ground devastated Marie at the deepest part of her. She placed her fingers at the pulse of her neck; it was weak but still there.

"Hang in there, Rachael. You're strong. You've got little Alo waiting for you at home. Just keep breathing." Marie ripped a piece of fabric from the hem of her skirt and wrapped it around the gash in Rachael's head to stanch the bleeding, praying to anyone who would listen to save her friend. Judson ran to where they were on the ground and took a position in front of Marie and Rachael to protect them.

"Cynthia Walvern," Anne-Marie said, the authority in her voice carrying over all the noise as if she had shouted.

"Cynthia is not in control. I am Cynder. Get it right! You wouldn't train Cynthia in her craft or treat her with the respect she deserved, so she came to me, and I am the one who trained her and developed her power, even as weak as it was. But when we joined together, we both became more powerful. I. Am. *Cynder.*"

Anne-Marie didn't even flinch or back down at anything Cynder said, whether it was true or not. She kept her expression neutral, her tone flat and in control. Roman Bishop as well as his father Rodavan came to stand on either side of her. Priscilla and Raffaele Augustine stood behind them, along with other Court members Lawrence Mills and Elsmed Fairchild. Marie couldn't figure out how they all knew where to find them. Marie figured it couldn't hurt to have a frost dragon and fae to assist just in case. No one knew what Cynder was capable of.

"I'm flattered you believed you could stop me with so few of you. Your collective power is still not enough." She laughed, unconcerned by their limited abilities.

"It is not just them." Marie stood with dirt-stained tear tracks on her face and blood smeared on her skirt. "Rachael fought for you, Cynthia. I know you can hear me. When I tell you, you fight with everything you have for control."

Cynder only laughed, although her image blurred in and out, which told Marie Cynthia had heard her. Cynder swayed on her feet, but she seemed unfazed by it. "It's only a matter of time. I just need a little more power to take over completely, and I will have it!" She moved toward Rachael and Judson, the closest of the witch magic. But Rachael, being weak and debilitated—on the brink of life—was an easy target.

Not on Marie's watch.

She jumped in front of both Rachael and Judson. Hearing his grumbled complaint behind her, she allowed her husband to move beside her.

"My dagger, Judson." She held out her hand expectantly. She knew he had it on him when they left. She remembered him using it in her dream—that couldn't have been a coincidence. He kept it hidden in the waistband at the back of his pants. He looked at her, confused.

"Marie? Don't do something stupid." He handed her the dagger.

"You know me better than that." She winked at him and took the dagger.

"That's what I'm afraid of," he whispered under his breath. "At least let me help."

She nodded. He was to be a part of it as well. "I read about it in the journal but didn't understand what it could mean until now. It's time for this witch hunter to rise up and take my place on behalf of all my family to come after me." She held the dagger out, but it was so small, Cynder laughed even harder.

Marie had to admit it didn't look good from the outside. She glanced to the others, who looked on with their own skepticism, except for Anne-Marie and Priscilla. The Bishops actually looked bored, and Lawrence looked mad. Elsmed—she couldn't tell what Elsmed was thinking, but if he could truly read minds, perhaps he already knew her plan. Unexpectedly, he crossed his arms and winked at her. Marie's heart soared. Anne-Marie and Priscilla both looked at her with faith and strength. Anne-Marie gave her a subtle nod. They would have her back.

"Cynder, this is your warning. Give up Cynthia and go back to where you came from!" Marie shouted.

"No. I earned my place with her. She gave up part of herself for me. Unless you're offering Judson, then I'll stay right where I am until I get something better!" she spat out. Her body jerked and moved at odd angles. She frowned and reared back as if surprised.

"So the little witch wants to play. You ungrateful wretch!" Cynder opened her hands and called lightning from the sky. She tossed it back and forth in her palms, gathering her strength and weakening whatever power Cynthia had left.

"Now, Marie," Anne-Marie quickly but quietly encouraged.

Marie stepped right in front of Cynder, took her dagger, and sliced her own hand, releasing a flow of blood.

"You didn't even try to stab me!" Cynder mocked, and cackled with sarcasm. "Is that it?"

"No. This is." Marie smeared her blood on the stone encased in the hilt of her dagger. The stone glowed, growing brighter and brighter. She held it in front of Cynder.

Everyone waited in anticipation for what would happen. If anything.

Marie closed her eyes and focused on the ability within her that was unique to her as a witch hunter. She found the spark of magic within Cynder she knew to be Cynthia's witch essence and pulled it toward her. As a witch hunter, she could pull the magical essence out of a witch and absorb it within herself— usually only if they were dead. That was how her brother Dante and the rest of the rogue witch hunters she left behind did what they did. But she had magic and her family's dagger on her side. Marie still felt guilt over what she was doing. After all, she chose to leave that way of life behind in order to have the life they now enjoyed. She may very well be asked to leave afterward, but she also knew it might be Cynthia's only chance. And for Rachael, she had to try.

"Nothing's happening! You're so foolish," Cynder chanted over and over. "Such a letdown." She shrugged her shoulders. "Oh well, no more playing. You're wasting my time." She released a shot of lightning toward Roman Bishop, but he quickly deflected it overhead into nearby trees with his own magic. Trees and branches fell around them.

Marie felt a surge of witch magic envelop them and wondered if one of the witches put a shield of protection around them. She barely had time to notice. She had to focus on what she was doing so she didn't damage Cynthia's soul and pull her essence too hard. Judson placed his hand over hers on the dagger, and she felt him release whatever magic he knew how to give.

"Witches, now! Cynthia, now!" Marie shouted under the strain of what she was doing. She felt the witches come together and share their magic, then direct it toward Cynder. She hoped that while she pulled on Cynthia, it gave the witches enough room to bind the demon with their magic and pull Cynder out. Her hope was that Cynthia would fight with everything she was to take control of her body, and while Marie pulled on her, she could push Cynder out from within. She had to find the perfect balance of pull and give to not pull Cynthia's soul completely out. She had never done it before, so she carefully teetered on the line, afraid of pulling too hard.

Marie could feel the tug-of-war within Cynthia. Tension grew and grew. Sweat beaded on Marie's forehead, then trickled down the sides of her face. A bundle of nerves grew tighter and tighter within her stomach.

A hand rested on her shoulder. She had the awareness Elsmed had come behind her. She didn't know what all his power was as a fae, but she felt strength and energy pour into her. He was lending her what he could.

"It's working. Keep going. She's almost free. I can sense it," he said in a low tone behind her.

And so she did. Finally, something snapped! A bright light shot out from her dagger. Cynthia fell to the ground unconscious. Marie flew back. Had Elsmed not been behind her, she would have landed on her backside. Judson reached for her hand to steady her. They ran to Cynthia lying on the ground. Elsmed placed his hand on her forehead and gave Marie a small smile and a reassuring nod. Marie was relieved, but she needed to see her eyes.

A scuffle sounded behind them. When Marie turned, she was surprised to find all the witches extending their hands toward a mass of darkness that grew larger than she thought was possible to hide within a young woman's body. They had Cynder —or the demon—bound and contained by their magic.

"Lawrence, the container!" Anne-Marie shouted.

Lawrence Mills came forward with a handmade box and opened the lid, placing it on the ground below the center of the dark mass. The witches chanted a spell while Anne-Marie guided the demon at the epicenter down into the box. By some magic, a void opened inside the box and sucked the darkness into it. An audible pop sounded when it was complete, taking the tension of the moment with it. Lawrence quickly shut the lid and locked it. Rodavan Bishop knelt down in front of the box and whispered a spell of his own that sealed the box.

"Rodavan, Roman, and Raffaele, please have a hellhound escort it back to where it belongs—in Hell," Anne-Marie directed.

Everyone breathed easier. Cynthia opened her emerald green eyes and cried. "She's gone. I don't feel the darkness anymore."

"No, you're free," Judson said, while Marie ran back to Rachael on the ground to tell her.

"We did it, Rach! Cynthia's free. You fought for her, and she's free," Marie said with tears and laughter. She stroked Rachael's head when she tried to open her eyes and smile.

"Thank you. She deserved to be free." Her breathing was shallow, but she had words to get out. "Take care of them for me. Promise me, Marie."

Marie lost all color in her face. "What? No, you take care of them. You're going to be fine."

"Promise me, Marie. You're my family. Raise Alo as your own. Promise."

Marie choked on her emotion, but said, "I promise."

"Love you, Marie."

"Love you too, Rach." Her eyelids fluttered closed, never to be opened again. Marie collapsed and sobbed.

# EPILOGUE

*M*onths after Rachael had passed on, Marie finally had the strength of heart and mind to not only leave their house but to officially open the Blackstone family vineyard. There was nothing like a beautifully decorated vineyard, surrounded by snow in the middle of December.

Ahote had become the most doting father to Alo and dove into the work he did on the vineyard to escape the pain of losing Rachael. It broke Marie's heart every time she saw them together, and yet at the same time, it healed a little bit each day. Everyone grieved her loss, especially at the Blackstone household, but also in the town. Rachael had been loved by many.

Priscilla Augustine took her loss extremely hard. She had later come to explain she had a vision of sorts of what would transpire after Judson's magic was unlocked. That was how the coven was prepared and showed up in the forest to help Marie against Cynder when they had. Priscilla saw it all unfold, and they followed each step, waiting to intervene until after someone had screamed *No*. Unfortunately, in her vision she only saw the parts they were to follow step by step. She never saw what happened to make Marie scream. She didn't know Rachael had put herself between Cynder and Judson and risked her life. But still she felt responsible, as if she should have known all things.

Marie didn't blame her. She was grateful Priscilla did get the vision and that the coven did come. Marie wished she'd been granted the foresight to see the entire picture, but nevertheless, Priscilla's vision saved the rest of them. If the members of the Court and coven hadn't interceded when they did, they all would be dead.

"Marie?" Hank, her father, called from the other side of the door.

"I'm ready," she replied. She had originally planned for a fall opening party, but after losing Rachael, they took more time, and instead, it was the heart of winter. Marie was okay with that. Winter was a beautiful time where they lived up in the mountains. It was colder than anything she had ever experienced, but she liked it. The sharp brisk air that stung her lungs when she inhaled deep made her feel alive amidst the pain. It reminded her life did go on and she was blessed to be among the living. She opened the door and stepped out.

Her father's smile warmed her heart. He said, "I wish your mama could see you now. She'd be so proud of you and the woman you have become, Marie Marcella Blackstone."

Marie reached up on her tiptoes and kissed his cheek. "Thanks, Dad. Now let's go get this vineyard officially opened to the public." She winked at him and giggled.

They didn't have far to go, since the party was right outside their home. They had placed paper bags filled with sand and small candles along the edges of the vineyard and surrounding an area designated as the dance floor. Also in strategic places were barrels of contained fires to help keep people warm. Her brother Rodney had made an attempt at decorating the buildings with some cutout paper flowers and snowflakes he had made with his adopted nephew, Alo. His technique needed some work, but the effort warmed her heart and made her smile.

Unlike Marie's dream, she would not walk down an aisle of

grapes at the vineyard, and she would not worry about the people being sucked into the darkness invading their town. Instead, she looked forward to the gathering of her family and friends to witness such a special time in the midst of the heartache and pain the last several years had held for everyone. Opening the vineyard would mark a turning point for the town, as it would bring in outside business, but also for them as a family.

She held the hem of her blue dress accompanied by light brown fur boots and a cream fur shawl to keep her warm. Her unruly blond hair was pinned high on her head, save the few pieces that refused to be bound.

Marie closed her eyes and slowly breathed in deep the crisp cold air, savoring every moment. They had done it. They built a new life, a new home, and a business to sustain them for years to come. She had planned and anticipated this very moment with Rachael by her side. Marie allowed a single tear to fall for her friend. Rachael would be missed, but Marie knew she was truly there in spirit.

When Marie lifted her head and opened her eyes, she gasped.

People. The area was full of people from the town. They had all been invited, but she didn't think they would come, due to recent events. They had created an aisle with unlit candles, leading her from the house to the outbuilding where they made the wine. Judson waited for her at a tall table they had made. Right where he was supposed to have been in the dream. On the table were glasses of all kinds, and the newly sealed bottles of wine ready for consumption.

All eyes were on her, waiting for her. And though it was the dead of winter, magically fireflies bobbed and weaved in the air above their heads. Judson extended his hand toward her, beckoning her to come. Her father led the way through the group of people—friends from the town. But unlike her dream, they were smiling, supportive, and happy to be there.

Just as she wanted at such a special celebration of their new life.

"I . . . I'm speechless," she said. "It's beautiful. Thank you. Thank you all for coming." She began to move toward Judson, ready to start the party.

"Oh, wait, please," Judson said out loud with a hint of embarrassed panic. He stood tall and closed his eyes, breathing deep and attempting to relax himself.

Marie looked quizzically at her father, but he simply shook his head, indicating he didn't know what Judson was up to. All at once, the candles lining the aisle burst into delicate little flames. He opened his eyes and smiled with pride. Marie laughed, ditched the traditional atmosphere, and ran the rest of the way into his arms.

"You're amazing," she whispered.

"You're amazing," he returned, and kissed her forehead.

A throat cleared. It was her brother Rodney. "Let's start this party! We're freezing our arses off out here."

The crowd laughed, and the evening turned into a magical moment. Wine freely flowed. Music played, and people danced. Though the loss was felt, it was important to enjoy the moments of life and love and togetherness.

Before the night was over, the Trents approached Judson and Marie with an item covered under a blanket. Marie was so excited, she couldn't wait to see what they had made for Judson, but when she glanced at Judson, he seemed equally excited. Before she could say anything, Gregory Trent interrupted.

He explained how both Judson and Marie had each gone to them to create an item for the other, so they put the ideas together. Instead of making two items, they had made one.

Charlotte Trent pulled off the blanket to reveal the most beautifully detailed wooden box Marie had ever seen. They both gasped in surprise.

"Oh my," Judson said, at the same time Marie said, "It's

beautiful." She couldn't help but run her fingers over the engraved scrollwork on the front.

Mr. Trent demonstrated by pulling open one of the drawers then clicking a lever and having the lid pop open. Deep red velvet lined the interior of the box. He showed them several other secret compartments and how to work the puzzle parts of it.

"This is truly amazing craftsmanship," Judson admired.

Mr. and Mrs. Trent left the box with them and bid them goodnight and congratulations on their vineyard, then left.

"This is perfect. I was thinking you could put your most special daggers or pieces of metal you work with in it," Marie admitted.

"And I hoped you could have a safe place for your dagger and journal when not in use."

"I think we should be able to accommodate all that and more in this box. There is more space than I thought there would be," Marie said with a huge smile.

"And I think we should keep it hidden in the secret vault in the armory in the basement to keep it safe," Judson said, deep in thought.

"But it's too pretty to hide away in the basement." Marie pouted.

"I agree, but I think it's important for future generations," he said, his face so serious that Marie agreed.

Anne-Marie and Sheriff Kasun approached Marie and Judson from the side so as not to draw too much attention to themselves. With them was Cynthia, looking extremely uncomfortable about being there.

"Marie and Judson?" Anne-Marie addressed them. "Cynthia wanted to say goodbye before she left."

Cynthia had been held by the coven in a magical prison of sorts to ensure the presence of darkness was completely gone. They continued to check her magic levels and were surprised to find she was currently a full witch, no longer only half. They could only conclude it had something to do with all the magic and the work Marie did on her soul simultaneously. But she had been growing stronger, and the uncertainty of it made them all uneasy, including Cynthia. During her time in the prison, she had told the Court where the other witches had been held. Sheriff Kasun and his pack found the handful of missing witches from their town, as well as a few others. Only one, from outside their town, was no longer alive, though the others had been completely drained of their magic and were in bad shape. After seeing the Luna Coven, they were all expected to make physical recoveries; sadly, the same could not be said for their magic.

"You're leaving?" Marie asked, surprised to just now learn this news.

"I am. My family is, too, actually. We decided we needed a fresh start somewhere else." She paused and hung her head. "Marie, I'm so sorry about Rachael. I . . . I . . ." Her words got choked in her throat.

Marie had no words, but hugged the girl and let her grieve and find forgiveness in that moment so they could all find some way to move forward.

After a minute or two, Marie pulled back with alarm. "I can't feel you, Cynthia. I mean, I can't feel your witch."

Anne-Marie placed her hand on Marie's forearm with understanding. "We bound her magic—at her request," she explained.

Shocked, Marie shook her head. "Why? Why would you do that?"

Cynthia shrugged. "I needed to start over. With everything in the past, I just wanted a chance to not worry about any of that. I'm really okay with it, Marie. But thank you for caring. Thank you for everything." She lunged forward and squeezed Marie so tight she couldn't breathe for a second.

"Goodbye, Cynthia."

Sheriff Kasun and Anne-Marie escorted her back out and to her family, who were apparently leaving that night. Marie felt bad, but she also felt relieved not to have to see Cynthia and have the reminder of what happened to Rachael every day. Marie truly didn't blame Cynthia, but she still wore the same face, and Marie couldn't unsee the petite girl throwing Rachael against the tree with her magic.

"You all right?" Judson asked, and kissed the top of her head.

Marie nodded. "But I could use a dance with my husband."

She smiled when he took her hand. Judson led Marie to the dance floor and spun her around a few times.

"What are you thinking, Marie?" Judson asked, placing his hands around her waist, drawing her close.

She sighed. "First of all, this is amazing. I'm so proud of the work everyone has done to make our vineyard a success." Her face turned down, and she gnawed on her bottom lip. When she looked back up at him, his warm gaze was so patient and understanding, she continued, "This is hardly the time or place, but I couldn't help but wonder now that Rachael isn't with us, what happens to the curse she put on Dante before we discovered this canyon?"

Judson frowned, deep in thought. He remembered how Rachael stood up to Dante when he faced off with Marie. To save Marie, Rachael cursed Dante in a way that would be the most detrimental to him. The curse would hide Marie and her family from his senses; he wouldn't be able to find them, no matter how hard he looked. And she cursed him to feel his humanity once again. However, by doing so, she tied her life to his. Meaning the curse would only remain in place as long as the one who cursed him remained alive. Now that Rachael no longer was among the living, Dante would regain his hunter side with a vengeance and come looking for Marie. Being where they were, and surrounded by the new wards their town was implementing, Marie would be hard to find. But Dante would never stop looking for her.

"Let's think on that another time. Tonight is for us." Judson encouraged her with a spin ending in a low dip.

They laughed and had the fun she had so anticipated for their opening ceremony. During a slower moment, she looked out at the people from the town who had come to celebrate with them. She watched Raffaele Augustine dip Priscilla to the point she giggled. The Bishops stood in the corner talking with Raffaele's brother while they drank punch she was pretty sure was laced with moonshine. The Trents' apprentice, Theodore Carver, took a turn on the dance floor with Betsy in his arms. Her father spun a couple different women around, and Marie laughed. Rodney and their cousins Caroline and Michael shoved special treats in their mouths. Other townspeople, including the Millses, Elsmed Fairchild and his wife, Ric and Gaby Kasun, Mihail and Irina Petran, Mr. and Mrs. Lancaster, and several others gathered about, mingling and having a good time. Ahote and Alo hesitated at first, but then she watched their faces light up when the father spun his son around in his arms and they allowed themselves to have fun. The sight was everything Marie wanted. She only wished Rachael could be there to see it too.

"I love you, Judson. I'm so grateful to have found a home with you," Marie said, and slowly kissed his lips.

Judson smiled from ear to ear. "I love you too, Marie. You did it."

"Did what?" She was suddenly confused.

"You followed your heart, chose who you wanted to be, found us a home, and called out the witch hunters to rise to the challenge of becoming something more."

Marie smiled. Yes, she did. She couldn't wait for the future generations of witch hunters to rise.

The dagger and its secrets remained in the family's protective possession for generations to come, and they continued to make weapons for the town. Judson and Marie weren't sure they would be able to have children with the seemingly combative traits between witch and witch hunter, but they did. Once their children—specifically daughters with the hunter's mark—began to demonstrate extreme challenges controlling their hunter side along with the witch magic, though, they asked the Luna Coven to bind the magic that flowed through them—at the children's request. The suppression was intended to be a blessing and a protection for their children and grandchildren. As the years went on and the generations continued, the knowledge of the magic in their veins was restricted, then lost . . . until there would eventually be one able to access the family journal in its entirety again.

~

We hope you enjoyed this story in the Legends of Havenwood Falls series featuring a variety of supernatural creatures. You may also want to read these other stories about the Blackstone witch hunters, all by Morgan Wylie (continue on for an excerpt of
*Reawakened*)
*Dawn of the Witch Hunters*
*Reawakened*
*Redefined*
*Rediscovered*

Books in the historical Legends of Havenwood Falls series:

*Lost in Time* by Tish Thawer
*Dawn of the Witch Hunters* by Morgan Wylie
*Redemption's End* by Eric R. Asher
*Trapped Within a Wish* by Brynn Myers
*Blood and Damnation* by Belinda Boring
*Fated Beginnings* by E.J. Fechenda
*Emeline* by Katie M. John
*Released From a Curse* by Brynn Myers
*A Pack of Lies* by Kallie Ross

*Kiss the Ashes* by Desiree Lafawn
*Hidden Truths* by Colleen Nye
*Wrath and Retribution* by Belinda Boring
*Changing Fate* by Char Webster
*Rise of the Witch Hunters* by Morgan Wylie
*The Drowning Bride* by Seven Jane

Also try the main Havenwood Falls series; the YA line, Havenwood Falls High; the darker, sexier side of town, Havenwood Falls Sin & Silk; and the local supernatural college, Sun & Moon Academy.

Stay up to date at www.HavenwoodFalls.com

Subscribe to our reader group and receive free stories and more!

# ABOUT THE AUTHOR

Morgan Wylie is an award-winning and *USA Today* Bestselling Author with several genres published from YA fantasy to adult paranormal romance, as well as other stories in between. Morgan published her first novel, *Silent Orchids,* one year after moving across the country with her family on a journey of new discovery. After an amazing three years in Nashville, Tennessee, and the release of two more books, Morgan and her family found their way back to the Northwest, where they now reside. With a collection of twelve-plus titles, she passionately pursues working every day with great optimism. Daily, Morgan continues to embrace all things: Mama, wife, teacher, and mediator to the many voices and muses constantly chattering inside her head, where it gets pretty loud!

You can find her and news on her books at the following:
MorganWylie.net
Morgan Wylie Books on Facebook
@MWylieBooks on Instagram (and Twitter)

# ACKNOWLEDGMENTS

Thank you for visiting the 1800s with me and the Blackstones again! Creating a collaborative world like this takes a village of amazing authors and an even more amazing leader supreme, and we have that in Kristie Cook, founder of Havenwood Falls. Thank you, Kristie, for letting us continue to play throughout all eras!

Thank you, Liz Ferry, for your time and your expertise! Thank you, Regina Wamba, for the beautiful covers and graphics you create! And thank you to Ang'dora Productions for allowing me the opportunity to work with you.

Thank you, Kristie Cook, for the collaboration with Anne-Marie Beaumont and the Luna Coven. Thank you, Randi Cooley Wilson, for the use of Rodavan and Roman Bishop, Eric Asher for the use of Charlotte and Gregory Trent as well as Theodore Carver and Betsy, Kallie Ross for the use of Ric and Gaby Kasun as well as the Kasun Pack, E.J. Fechenda for the use of Elsmed Fairchild and his wife, Kristen Yard for the use of Martha Daryn and the Green Coven, and Amy Hale for the use of Lawrence Mills and family. It is always an honor to get to collaborate with such amazing and generous authors. Thank you!

# AN EXCERPT

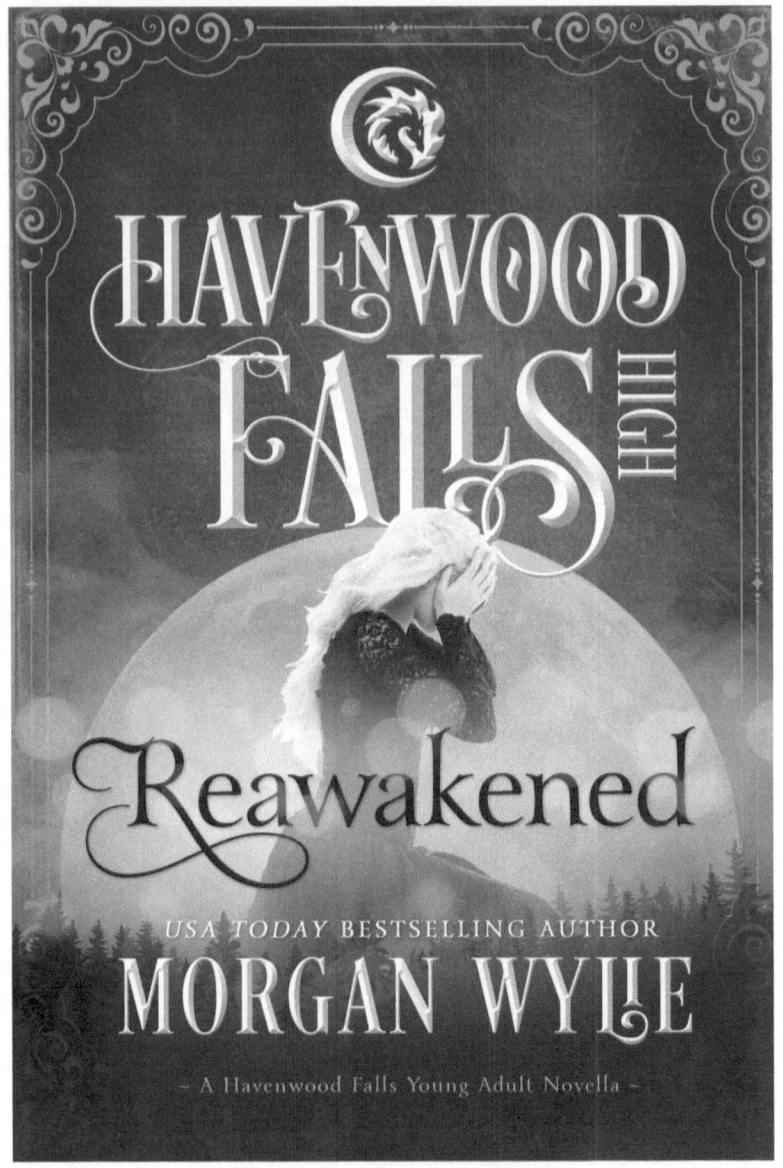

HAVENWOOD FALLS HIGH

Reawakened

USA TODAY BESTSELLING AUTHOR

MORGAN WYLIE

~ A Havenwood Falls Young Adult Novella ~

*Welcome to Havenwood Falls, a small town in the majestic mountains of Colorado. A town where legacies began centuries ago, bloodlines run deep, and dark secrets abound. A town where nobody is what you think, where truths pose as lies, and where myths blend with reality. A place where everyone has a story. Including the high schoolers. This is only but one . . .*

Like all young witch hunters in Havenwood Falls, seventeen-year-old Macy Blackstone has been spelled to control her killer instincts. When she's reawakened too early, though, her world flips upside down.

Daughter to the Blackstone witch hunters' matriarch, Macy should have known what was coming, but her mother hadn't prepared her. Overwhelmed with the surge of energy from the new moon coupled with a solar eclipse, she's unable to handle the new sensations, and she flees town. To her surprise, she discovers an entire family branch of witch hunters living nearby. Only, the more she gets to know them, the more she learns about their dark intentions for both the witches and the Blackstones of Havenwood Falls.

Gallad Augustine, witch and boyfriend extraordinaire, possesses powerful magic, but Macy took off too soon for him to help her. Now, as her soul mate, his connection to her heart may be the only way for anyone to reach her.

Macy has one moon cycle—twenty-eight days—to uncover the witch hunters' plans and return home before the town's wards wipe her memory permanently and she forgets everything about her family, her home, and her one true love. And if she can't remember them, she won't be able to save them.

# REAWAKENED

## BY MORGAN WYLIE

Most seventeen-year-olds about to enter their senior year of high school enjoyed every last bit of their summer break. Some even went on vacations. Not me—Macy Blackstone, witch hunter. All I wanted to do was forget the title and be normal at least for a day, but apparently that day was not today.

Nearing the end of August in Havenwood Falls, Colorado, the weather had already began to change—not that it ever stayed any particular temperature for long. Up in the mountains especially, fall came earlier than in the lower elevations. The nights grew chilly earlier, and mornings like this one reminded me what I loved about fall.

Cozy in my oversized, chunky cable-knit wrap sweater, I snuggled into the corner of a large outdoor sectional sofa in front of a giant rock fireplace. Stretching out my legging-clad legs, complete with warm Uggs on my feet, I sighed with contentment. I watched the town come to life below me while I slowly sipped from the steaming mug of coffee in my hand. Rays from the sunrise streaked down to touch the edge of our deck, stretching as far as the fire pit and the uncovered section of deck. The reverse would happen just the same again at sunset. Tipping my head up, I closed my eyes, absorbing warmth from the sun's kiss as it crept up my face, inching as far as the roof above would allow it.

"Beautiful, isn't it?" My mom's voice floated from the doorway separating the kitchen from the outside living area.

"It is," I answered, looking back at her. My mom, Lilith Blackstone, was a beautiful woman, appearing in her mid-forties —though she was actually a bit older. For a human, she looked forty-five, but as a hunter, she was still relatively young at seventy-eight years old. Most of the women in my family were hunters—witch hunters to be exact, though we didn't actively hunt witches. My mom was descended from the founding Blackstone family, a strong lineage of witch hunters. She also held a seat on the Court of the Sun and the Moon as the representative and matriarch for our entire family.

"Are you seeing Gallad today?" she asked, moving toward the railing, carrying her own steaming mug.

"I'm supposed to meet him at the vineyard pretty soon, actually." I checked the time on my phone.

Her eyes were on me, watching me, the weight of her assessing stare boring into me. Turning to face her, I couldn't place her expression. Was she upset? She seemed more questioning than anything else.

"Is something wrong, Mom?"

"How are you feeling?" she returned, avoiding my question.

"Um, fine thanks, but don't think I am that easily diverted. What's up?"

Coming over to me, she placed her hand on the back of my neck, now free from my silky blonde locks since I piled them on top of my head in a messy bun that morning. "How is your injury?"

"It's much better since the witches gave us that healing salve to put on it." Reflexively, I touched the back of my neck as well after she pulled away. "There's some scabbing where the stupid tree limb tore my flesh off, but otherwise I think it's good. See?"

I pulled the neck of my sweater down, and tugged my T-shirt back for her to see it.

In a reckless attempt to be normal, I had climbed a tree and tried to jump to an adjacent tree like some damn spider-monkey wannabe. The new tree didn't want to be my friend and wouldn't let me grab hold of it until I had slid down part way, taking my flesh off as I went.

"Your hunter marking looks to be untouched. However, your protection tattoo got a bit roughed up. Did you have Saundra Beaumont look at it like I asked?"

Saundra Beaumont sat on the high council of the Luna Coven, making her one of the most powerful witches in town.

Since I was born, my parents and the Court knew what I would become based on a stupid skin discoloration on the back of my neck in the shape of a cluster of small stars. All hunters were born with it, like a birthmark—or a beacon of doom.

"Yes, Mom. She said it looked fine, and I shouldn't have any issues with the wards within my tattoo. Addie looked at it, too. She said she'd need to touch up a few of the lines but would wait until the skin was fully healed. They both agreed the tattoo held enough magic that it shouldn't be an issue to wait until it was time for the permanent one."

In Havenwood Falls, all the supernatural residents received a tattoo infused with magic. The markings were there for not only our protection, but also for the town's. They protected each individual race, but also helped temper and conceal magic from our human residents, who made up about half of our population. Visitors also had to register with the Court of the Sun and Moon to receive a temporary tattoo for the duration of their stay.

As I grew older, into double digits, the Luna Coven placed a magical, invisible-to-the-eye marking in the shape of a crescent moon with a dragon right below my birthmark. The tattoo was a temporary marking intended to suppress any hunter tendencies until I turned eighteen. According to our traditions as witch hunters, at the age of eighteen we go through a ceremony, committing ourselves to abide by the rules and laws of Havenwood Falls. Hunters can choose for themselves then if they are going to go out on their own, never to return to Havenwood Falls, or become a suppressed member of the Blackstone family and town at large. Good options, right? Normal human high schoolers didn't have to deal with that kind of crap. Choice made and ritual completed, we then receive the permanent tattoo of an adult, thus becoming an official citizen of Havenwood Falls.

"Speaking of which, Macy, I need to speak with you about your upcoming birthday and marking ceremony." A slight edge laced Mom's words, anticipating my reply.

I sighed. This was an old conversation. My eighteenth birthday was coming up the beginning of October.

"Mom, we've talked about this. I still have some time. Can we not talk about it yet? School is starting soon and I want to enjoy the last of summer. Since I can't go anywhere interesting, I want to try to be as normal as possible while I still can." Even I could hear the bitterness and whiny petulance in my tone.

"Macy," she practically growled enough to rival one of the Kasun wolves. The Kasuns were not only the largest werewolf pack in Havenwood Falls, but their alpha, Ric Kasun, was also the town sheriff. "You have put this off for too long. The ceremony will happen, and you need to be prepared. There are things you should know and things to prepare for."

Jumping up from my no-longer-quiet space, I faced her. Then she did something I was not expecting. Moving to the side, she revealed another woman standing behind her in the kitchen, watching the interaction with a frown. Looking from the new arrival back to my mother, I scowled.

"You brought Grandma into this?" Fury pulsed through my veins. I loved my grandmother, and I was normally a reasonable —okay, *somewhat* reasonable—person, but she went behind my back like I needed some kind of intervention.

Eva Blackstone, aka Grandma, was regularly brought in when my mom didn't get her way—at least it looked that way to us kids, my two brothers and myself.

"Now, Macy, be rational. There are many details to attend to and your orientation to complete," Grandma chided from the kitchen, beckoning me inside. Tall, slender, and confident, my grandmother held an air of regality and pride. Her hair had been a fierce blond bob since I could remember, mirroring the same edge in her personality.

"This is my last year of high school, and I'll spend most of it as an official Blackstone hunter. I just want to spend the rest of my summer as an irresponsible teenager. Is that too much to ask?" I huffed and folded my arms across my chest.

"Yes, it is," Grandma said flatly. "You have a responsibility to this family and this town. It is time you owned up to it."

I put my mug in the sink and took several slow drags of air, cooling my growing temper.

"Macy, nothing changes once you are marked. It's all in your head," Grandma added.

I shot a glance toward my mom still standing in the doorway. Her gaze was off in the distance, watching the rising sun or something else farther away, locked in the recesses of her mind. Distracted, she finally felt my stare and looked back to me. I frowned.

"I don't know about that, Grandma," I whispered. My mom definitely had times when she was off, but lately, it had been more obvious. She was hiding something, but I didn't know what.

"Oh that's ridiculous, child. You have until the end of summer and then you will take your place in this town as a Blackstone hunter or . . ."

I spun my head in her direction, mouth open wide. "There's an 'or' in your sentence?"

"Macy, you know the rules of Havenwood Falls. If a witch hunter will not choose to be permanently marked, they cannot remain a resident here," my mother interjected. "And because of the memory wards around the borders, whoever chooses not to stay and follow the laws will forget everything about Havenwood Falls, including their family."

"I know the laws, but I don't need my family threatening me with them either." My heart suddenly felt heavy and sad. I knew they didn't mean to hurt me, but still they did. I grabbed my messenger bag off the counter and moved swiftly through the large, rustic yet modern kitchen-dining-great room toward the front door.

"Where are you going, young lady?" Grandma's voice echoed through the room.

"I'm meeting Gallad at the vineyard, then I have to go into the square to pick up my check at Broastful Brews." I sighed, then schooled my voice to an acceptable tone. "I'm sorry, I just need some space. I'll be back later."

"Let her go, Mom. I'll talk to her again later." My mom's voice reached me before I opened the front door.

Purchase *Reawakened* where books are sold.